NOVELS FOR ADULT LEARNERS

Three Wise Men

KATE FERRIS

CENTRE FOR CURRICULUM, TRANSFER AND TECHNOLOGY
VICTORIA, BRITISH COLUMBIA

THREE WISE MEN

by Kate Ferris

This novel has been written especially for adults learners improving their reading skills. The development and production was funded by the Province of British Columbia, Ministry of Education, Skills and Training and Human Resources Development Canada, National Literacy Secretariat.

Project coordination: Centre for Curriculum, Transfer and Technology
Design and production coordination: Bendall Books
Cover design and illustration: Bernadette Boyle

CANADIAN CATALOGUING IN PUBLICATION DATA

Ferris, Kate.
Three wise men
(Novels for adult learners)
ISBN 0-7718-9489-9
1. High interest-low vocabulary books. 2. Readers (Adult) I. Centre for Curriculum, Transfer and Technology. II. Title. III. Series.
PS8561.E7T57 1997 428'.62 C97-960062-6
PR9199.3F4T57 1997

ORDER COPIES FROM

Marketing Department
Open Learning Agency
4355 Mathissi Place
Burnaby, BC, Canada V5G 4S8
Telephone: 604-431-3210
Toll-free: 1-800-663-1653
Fax: 604-431-3381
Order Number: VA0195

CONTACT FOR INFORMATION

Centre for Curriculum, Transfer and Technology
5th Floor, 1483 Douglas Street
Victoria, BC, Canada V8W 3K4
Telephone: 250-387-6065
Fax: 250-387-9142

ALSO IN THE SERIES, NOVELS FOR ADULT LEARNERS

THE BUCKLE by Don Sawyer
CROCODILES AND RIVERS by Don Sawyer
FROZEN TEARS by Don Sawyer
THE MAILBOX by Kate Ferris
THE SCOWLING FROG by Kate Ferris

Distributed By:
Grass Roots Press
Toll Free: 1-888-303-3213
Fax: (780) 413-6582
Web Site: www.literacyservices.com

ACKNOWLEDGEMENTS

This book was written in consultation with the Adult Basic Education classes at the Selkirk College Learning Centre in Nakusp, B.C. The meetings with the students were immensely enjoyable and fruitful. I thank them all.

Special thanks go to Patty Bossort, who initiated this project; also to Richard Allin, Susan Crichton; and to Craig Anderson at Selkirk College.

I would also like to thank Audrey Thomas, Yvette Souque, Dennis Anderson, and JoAnne Pasquale and their respective agencies.

Last but not least, I would like to thank three great guys: Glen, Hank and Nick. Their adventures in New York provided a basis for the fictional story which follows.

Mr. Baxter

Mr. Baxter drew back the curtain and peered down at 7th Avenue. It was the first day of December. For the month of December, the city of New York changed for the good. Beggars made more money. People smiled more. Strings of coloured lights blinked from awnings and windows.

Mr. Baxter pressed his forehead against the cold windowpane. It was all building up to that terrible day, that one terrible day.

Below, the street bustled with traffic. Even early on a Sunday morning, horns honked, brakes screeched. The faint scream of a siren grew louder. And here it came, louder and louder. The screaming ambulance cut a path through the cars and trucks. "Poor soul."

Mr. Baxter looked across 7th Avenue, at the empty lot. He spent a good part of his day staring at that empty lot. Oh, it wasn't completely empty. The lot was a storage place for city work crews. It was surrounded by a high chain-link fence with barbed wire strung along the top. And inside the fence there were barrels and cables and coils of plastic pipe lying around.

But it was empty enough. Staring down, his mind could wander. He was 70 years old. And today was the first day of a month that he dreaded all year.

1

Sunday, December 1

8 A.M.

The tiny airport bus sped along the expressway. The driver seemed to aim for every pothole in the road. The luggage in the back bounced from side to side. The heater was broken, and all seven passengers rode bundled up in their coats. A black woman in the middle seat was lucky enough to be wearing gloves, a wool scarf, and a fur hat.

The three men squeezed together in the back seat weren't so lucky.

"It's cold. Where are our hats? Did you remember to pack them, Glen?"

"They're in my suitcase. No way I'd leave those hats behind, not our special hats. Those hats are going to bring us lots of business. Right, Nicki?"

He was answered with a nod, and a husky, “Yeah.”

The airporter hit another pothole. Most of the passengers were thrown against each other. The luggage slid back and forth. The three men in the back seat only swayed together, they were so tightly packed. The two smaller men sat on either side of the larger, heavier man.

“No way I’d forget those hats.”

The little bus lurched again.

“Holy smoke! Don’t they fix the roads here?”

The woman in the fur hat turned her head. “They’ve been fixing the expressway for five years.”

“You must be a New Yorker, am I right?”

The woman nodded.

“Me and my buddies here, we’re from Canada.”

“Oh?” with a faint smile of interest. “It’s cold up there, I hear.” As she spoke, puffs of frozen air rose from her mouth.

“By the way, I’m Glen.” His round face was eager and open. His deep-set eyes took everything in. He turned to his left. “This is Hank.”

Hank smiled a shy smile beneath his handlebar mustache. Then he turned to look out the window, exposing the bald spot at the back of his head.

“And on my right here, this is Nicki.”

“Hey, how ya doing?” Nick’s voice was low and warm. He extended his small but strong hand to the woman.

Glen cut in. “We’re from a small village in British Columbia.” He waved towards the window. “And now look—”

They were crossing a bridge. The skyline of New York offered itself to view. Glen leaned forward, talking fast in his excitement. "Ma'am, how many people live in New York City? How many would you say?"

"I don't really know," said the black woman.

"A million? Two million?"

"It's over eight million," offered a man in the forward seat.

Glen grinned. "Guess how many people live in our village. Go on. Just guess."

The woman laughed. "I don't have any idea."

"Only 600. Six hundred people." Glen gripped the back of her seat as he stared out the side window. His dark hair was cropped close at the back of his thick ruddy neck. There was only a touch of grey at his temples.

Nick was also staring out at the city. "Yeah, man, what a trip." He shook his head in wonder. His grey frizzy hair was pulled back from his high forehead and tied in a ponytail with a strip of leather. His face was strong-boned, and his nose had a slight hook at the bridge. His dark eyes and his skin shone with health. "This is some place, man," he murmured. "Some place."

"We're here on an adventure," said Glen, his eyes shining with excitement.

"And to make money," was Hank's quiet comment to himself.

The driver yelled over his shoulder. "Who's getting out at Spring Street and 24th?"

The black woman held up her gloved hand, "That's my stop."

The airporter slowed, pulling over to the curb. The woman

gathered her coat around her bulk, and hung her purse over her arm. "Thank you." She stepped down, her elbow guided by Nick.

One by one, the passengers got off at their stops. The back door of the airporter would open wide. Exhaust fumes would pour in while the driver pulled out suitcases, set them on the curb, and took his fare.

Now the bus sped down 7th Avenue, picking up speed. The driver wanted to beat the red light. At the last minute, he hit the brakes. The three men in the back seat were thrown forward. "Whoa!"

With the green light the little bus lurched forward. It wove between yellow taxicabs as it sped down the avenue.

"The guy's a maniac," muttered Hank.

Glen gripped the back of the seat ahead. "No one's staying in their own lane."

"Seventh Avenue and Greenwich!" barked the driver.

"That's us," cried Glen, starting up from the seat.

Nick laid a hand on Glen's arm. "Take it easy. Let the man stop."

"Where are we supposed to wait?" asked Hank. His brow furrowed. "Which corner?"

Nick lifted his arm and pointed out the window on Hank's side. Leather fringe hung down from the sleeve of his suede jacket. "Over there, in front of that empty lot with the chain-link fence."

The three men now began their wait at the southeast corner of the intersection. All their possessions lay on the sidewalk at their feet.

Two knapsacks, and a suitcase tied with a rope. Plus their sleeping bags.

Their breath rose in clouds. Hank stamped his feet. He hugged himself to keep warm. His wide mustache became frosted from his breath.

"Hank, move over here!" Glen waved him closer. "There's warmer air coming up from these grates in the sidewalk."

A faint *clackety-clackety* sounded beneath their feet. It rose quickly to a roar. The two men stared down at the grate. Below, the rush and rattle of a subway train died away.

Nick was bent over a trash basket at the curb. "Hey, we got some twine here." He pulled it out, winding it around his hand. "Twine always comes in handy when you're living on the street." He touched his forehead with his finger, to show that he was using his brains. "We gotta get into survival mode. This is New York City."

Glen joined him at the curb. A passing truck belched a cloud of exhaust over the curb. "Phew." Glen made a face and turned away. He'd put on his Christmas hat made of green fleece, with earflaps hanging down. Facing away from the street, Glen now studied the big billboard high above the empty lot. A siren screamed from far off, coming closer and closer.

"Holy jeez!" Glen jumped at the grinding crash of metal against metal behind him. "What happened?" he cried, turning around.

Out on 7th Avenue, a yellow cab had twisted sideways to a stop. Steam rose from under its buckled hood. The avenue was a one-way street with six lanes, and traffic still flowed around the stranded cab. Its driver stood by its opened door. While traffic sped past, the cabbie shook his fist in the air, shouting curses.

Glen rolled his eyes and cast a glance along the sidewalk in both directions. "I hope no ladies can hear that."

"There's just us," came a voice, and laughter. Two young women with shaved heads were walking arm in arm towards the corner. They wore black leather jackets, black jeans, and black leather boots. One of the women wore a silver ring in her nostril.

They stepped off the curb without waiting for the light.

Glen stared after them. It was a dangerous intersection. There weren't just two streets crossing here—there were three, coming in at different angles.

But no one seemed worried. Other New Yorkers were walking out into the traffic. They dodged the cars and trucks that sped past.

A tow truck had arrived. A policeman now waved the traffic around the smashed taxicab.

But Glen's attention was elsewhere. His stomach was growling as he pulled a thick heavy sweater over his head. "Dig into your pockets, boys," he called from inside the sweater. "I'm going over to that pizza place across the street. We need breakfast." In a moment his red, cheerful face emerged. The sweater had a pattern of reindeer and big snowflakes. "My sister knit this." He smoothed the sweater over his round stomach.

Watching Glen hurry away, Hank turned to Nick. "How long do you think we'll have to wait? I thought the van was supposed to be here when we arrived." He checked his wristwatch. "Are you sure this corner is the right one? There's no chance of a mix-up?"

"It'll happen, man. All in good time."

Hank frowned, and squinted up at the sky. It was a pale, cold blue. He was dressed for winter, with long underwear next to his skin. He wore hiking boots and red wool knee socks. The socks reached up to meet green wool knickers. Red suspenders stretched up over the shoulders of his black sweater. He looked like a slender, handsome elf—an elf with a handlebar mustache.

Church bells rang out over the noise of the traffic. Their ringing notes seemed to hover in the bare branches of the only tree in sight—a big oak on the other side of Greenwich Avenue.

And here came Glen, trotting back in his reindeer sweater and wearing a big grin. "I told the guy about my pizza parlor back home!"

He handed out the slices of pizza on their squares of waxed paper. "The guy's Italian. He told me his secret. He always sprinkles a little corn meal on his pans first, to get a crisper crust." He took an eager bite of his pizza slice.

At the smell and sight of food, pigeons circled in the air. Several landed on the sidewalk. They approached with jerky steps.

Soon more pigeons landed, to gather around Nick. He was an easy mark. "Hey man, you hungry?" With jerky steps, the cooing birds closed in around his feet. Nick was wearing high brown moccasins that matched his fringed jacket. The moccasins reached high on his calves and were wrapped with leather thongs.

He was tearing off bits from his pizza slice and tossing them to the sea of pigeons. "Yeah, we're gonna be friends..."

Hank kept his pizza to himself. He leaned against the chain-link fence taking small, slow bites. Behind him, above the vacant lot, the huge billboard announced:

Perry Street Theater—Proudly Lesbian-Owned

But the signs on the stores across 7th Avenue had already caught his attention.

The Village Vanguard

Wasn't that a famous jazz club? It didn't look very famous. There was a dirty-looking awning, and the entrance was down a few steps from street level. Hank chewed his pizza.

Quik-Stop Dry Cleaners – One-Hour Service

Hah! They always say one hour, and it always takes two or three days to get your cleaning back.

At the next sign he chuckled, his breath rising in a foggy wisp. "Listen to this, you guys!" Hank read the sign aloud:

Ear Piercing

Your Choice: With Pain, or Without Pain

Above the sign, a fire escape zig-zagged up the side of the building. Hank's gaze followed the metal stairs up, and up. Without taking his eyes off the building, he called out, "Glen, come over here."

"What? What is it?"

"I'm not going to point. But there's an old guy at the window up there, across the street. Above the sign that says 'With Pain or Without Pain.' Do you see him? Up on the third floor. He's looking at us with binoculars. I think he's been watching us ever since we got here."

"Yeah, I see him. He probably thinks we're just three more bums on the street." Glen lifted his arm and waved a friendly wave.

But the man at the third floor window drew back, as if startled to be seen.

Mr. Baxter

Mr. Baxter lowered his binoculars and stepped back from the window. For a moment he felt the old excitement. Something was going on across the avenue. He had an instinct about these things. From years of habit, he suspected the worst. This was natural in his line of work. That is, in what had been his line of work, for 40 years. Mr. Baxter was retired now.

He sighed. Why fool himself? Nothing was going on across the street. He set the binoculars back on top of the TV.

Once again, his thoughts were pulled back to the past. It was a past that he would rather forget. He usually managed to put it out of his mind for 11 months of the year. But the month of December was different. Every morning, he woke to the knowledge of what he'd done. Or rather, what he'd failed to do, that December, all those years ago.

He bent his grey head to his hands. Why had he been such a fool?

2

An Hour Later

An hour later a brown van drew up at the curb. The driver rolled down the window. In a thick New York accent he yelled, "Where ya from?"

"What do you mean?" asked Hank.

"I asked you where ya from. Don't give me any trouble."

Glen piped up, "We're from Canada."

And Hank pointed to his own head. He wore a red wool cap, with "CANADA" in white letters across the brow, ending in a big white maple leaf. "Can't you read?"

The driver turned off his engine, set the brake, and climbed out. He left the van's door open. "It's all yours." He blew his nose in a wrinkled rag. He put the rag back in his pocket, and started to walk away.

"Hey man, hold on," cried Nick. "Where's the keys?"

The driver stopped, and turned slowly around. "I keep the

keys—on orders from the boss." Turning to go, he jerked his head toward the van. "That's your Home Sweet Home for the next month."

Glen's earnest voice could be heard calling from inside the van. "There's only two foam pads in here! And there's three of us."

"Relax, Glennie." Nick leaned in at the open door. "Two beds are all we're gonna need at one time. One of us has gotta stay awake to keep watch."

"It smells pretty musty in here." Glen's voice echoed in the hollow space. "Hey! There's a heater here in the back." He brought it out, and set it down on the sidewalk grate.

The small electric heater looked like something set out for the garbage truck.

"There's only one problem." Hank's face was pinched from the cold, his nose was red above his mustache.

"What's that?"

"How are we going to plug it in?"

Their problem was soon to be solved.

A man was approaching across the sidewalk. "Excuse me." He looked to be about Glen or Hank's age—40 or so. He was wearing a heavy army surplus coat, yet he shivered. His nose was running. When he spoke, it was with a sleepy southern drawl. "You-all got a cigarette?"

Glen laid a kindly hand on the man's shoulder. "Buddy, you're already smoking a cigarette."

"Oh." He seemed to wake up. With dirty fingers he removed the cigarette from his mouth. He looked at it. "So I am." He placed the cigarette back between his chapped lips. He squinted up at Glen. "Might you have a cigarette anyway?"

"Gee, no, I'm sorry." Glen spread his palms out. "None of us smoke, you see."

"That's too bad." But the fellow didn't move on. He stood there, shivering in his jacket. His pale eyes were half-closed. His reddish hair was matted and dirty.

"You look pretty beat," offered Glen.

The man nodded. "The cops on the subway kept waking me up all last night. And you have to keep one eye open for muggers." He hitched up the pack on his back. "They'll steal your stuff."

"The subway? You rode the subway all night?"

"That's the cheapest way to keep warm."

"Speaking of keeping warm..." Hank had squatted down by the heater. He was frowning. "We'll need a long cord." He glanced over to Greenwich Avenue. "And we'll need somewhere to plug it in."

The stranger brightened. "You-all need a cord?" A fit of coughing and hacking stopped him for a moment. When he recovered, there was a look of hope in his pale eyes. "How long would you like this cord to be?"

Hank looked around. "Well, I'm not sure. I'd say at least 100 feet, maybe 150."

The stranger blew out a stream of smoke and then hurried away with a sense of purpose.

When he returned, there was a sleepy smile on his face. The

coils of an electric cord were looped over his arm. He dumped the cord by the little heater.

Nick eyed the cord with suspicion. "That's great, man, don't get me wrong..." He stopped himself, then continued in a gentler tone. "Tell me, where you from? You sound like you're from one of the southern states."

"I'm from the state of Texas." The man's smile widened. There were several teeth missing.

"And what's your name?"

"Eddy."

"Eddy. Texas Eddy. That's great, man, that's great. But here's the thing, Eddy. We don't want any stolen goods."

Eddy's smile faded. "That cord isn't stolen." His trembling fingers reached up to his cigarette. "There's no need to steal in this city. Anything you can imagine, people throw it away."

"Sorry, no offense, right? Hey, let's shake hands. Yeah, that's great."

Eddy's voice took on an edge of pride. "I can get you anything you need. I know where everything is. If I don't know where it is, I know where to look."

Nick and Hank and Glen exchanged glances. Then Hank asked, "How much for the cord?"

Eddy sniffed. He took a deep drag on his cigarette. He wiped his runny nose on his sleeve. "Four bucks."

The cord proved to be 200 feet long. It was a heavy-duty cord, with a three-prong plug. And the reason that it had been thrown away? The flaw was a small cut in the rubber in one place. But that could be mended with tape.

Hank pulled out his wallet. "We'll take it."

Glen's eyes narrowed. "What about some black plastic? Or a tarp? We've got to build ourselves a shelter here."

"I thought we were going to live in the van."

Nick cut in. "The van is just to sleep in. We need a place I can *cook*… Hey Eddy, my man. Think you can find me a campstove? A two-burner?"

"And we'll need a hammer," added Hank.

Glen joined in. "How about a lamp, so we can sit and read?"

By now, Eddy's cigarette burned dangerously close to his lip. "You-all want plastic…" He squinted into the distance, as if in his mind's eye he saw a nice big roll of it. "Tarp, campstove… lamp." He bent down and picked up a cigarette butt from the sidewalk. He lit this fresh butt from the ashy stub stuck to his lower lip. Then he flicked off the old cigarette with his tongue. It wasn't a very healthy looking tongue. It was coated white. The truth was, Eddy didn't smell very good. And as he walked away, Hank finally drew a deep breath in relief.

"You think he'll be back?"

Within a few hours, Eddy had earned himself $20. And he'd told them where to find scrap lumber with plenty of good nails in it. "Go down Greenwich two blocks. You-all can find a big green dumpster on the north side of the street." He folded his money together.

Nick pointed at the bills. "Tell me the truth now, Eddy. You gonna use that for drugs?"

Eddy's pale eyes met Nick's dark stare. He spoke as if insulted. "I don't do drugs."

"Well, what is it? You gonna drink up that money?"

"If I drink I get a headache." Eddy stuffed the bills into his army jacket. "I plan to rent a room and catch some sleep." He had never stopped shivering. "I might buy myself a steak sandwich."

Glen laughed. "And a pack of cigarettes?"

"No..." Eddy eyed a couple walking past. "I don't buy cigarettes." The woman tossed her half-smoked cigarette to the gutter. Eddy walked over and picked up the burning cigarette. He pinched its glowing end, and slipped the butt into his pocket.

By two o'clock that afternoon, the three men had nailed together a small hut from scrap lumber. From the roof of the brown van, they slanted down some old two-by-fours. These rafters they covered with a blue plastic tarp. They secured the tarp with the twine that Nick had fished from the trash basket.

Black plastic covered the two walls on either side. But the front of the little shelter was open to the sidewalk and people passing by. Some of the people looked in, then walked on. Some stopped to watch Hank swing his hammer, and to offer him advice.

And some people didn't even glance over as they strode past. They were used to seeing strange things on the streets of their city. What they saw now was just three more homeless men, building a shelter that the police would soon order them to tear down.

The sun had risen as high in the sky as it could on that winter day. It beamed down its pale warmth.

The work had warmed Nick's blood. He paced, feeling restless. Finally he dug around in his backpack—and pulled out his flute. The flute was made up of nine reeds placed side by side. Each reed was a different length, which meant that it sounded a different note. It was called a pan-flute, being named after Pan, the ancient god of nature.

Nick slipped the flute into the pocket of his fringed jacket.

Hank looked up. He stopped hammering. He was making a table out of an old door found in the dumpster. "Where are you going?" he asked Nick in a worried voice. "What if the trees come when you're gone?"

"I gotta give Kate a call."

"But I thought you two broke up. I thought she wasn't talking to you."

"She's not. But, hey..." Nick patted his pocket. "I got my flute."

Nick headed over to 8th Avenue. There was bound to be a phone booth over there. As he walked he whistled, with his chin held high. Even at age 55, there was a bounce to Nick's step. It was as if he had more energy than his slight body could contain. He could feel the hum of the city in his veins. He felt lucky. This was going to be his lucky day, no doubt about it.

The bell on his Christmas hat jingled at the back of his mind. He pulled it off and stuffed it into his other pocket as he strode along. With both hands he smoothed back his grey frizzy hair. His lucky day.

The phone booth over at 8th Avenue was already in use. Inside, a kid leaned with his back against the glass. Graffiti had been sprayed all over the sides of the phone booth. The marks and wiggles spelled out people's names, or strange messages. Nick walked around to the other side of the booth. He tried to catch the kid's eye. Pacing back and forth, he jingled the coins in his pocket. But the boy didn't really see him. There were tears running down his cheeks as he pleaded into the phone. Nick lifted his hand in apology. "Sorry, take your time, no hurry."

Killing time, Nick strolled along the sidewalk. A tall black man limped past on one crutch. *Jangle jangle jangle*. He was shaking coins in a tomato can. The clatter hurt Nick's ears. The beggar paused. His skin was strangely grey. Nick looked up into the man's eyes. The man stared back. Nick knew he was supposed to put money into the tomato can. He dug in his pocket, and brought up a couple of Canadian quarters. "I guess you can't use these." The man didn't even blink an eye, he simply turned on his crutch and limped on. The *jangle jangle jangle* carried for a block or more.

Nick turned around and strolled back. He stopped in front of a woman who sat cross-legged on a blanket. She was selling used clothing and books.

Nick glanced over at the phone booth—still busy.

"Hey, what you got here?" He picked up a little pocket dictionary from the blanket and thumbed through its pages. There sure were a lot of words he didn't know. He glanced around at all the books spread out on the blanket.

Nick didn't remember ever having read an entire book. After

10 minutes of reading his body would get jumpy, restless. He'd have to get up and go chop some firewood or something. Seeing all these books, he thought of Kate. In his opinion she read more books than was good for a human being. In fact, right at this very moment, she was probably reading. Back in Calgary she'd be reading the Sunday paper in bed. Nick pictured her in bed. Kate was a classy lady, a college professor, very smart. Nick sighed. *No getting around it. Kate, she's a beautiful woman.*

As Nick paid for the little dictionary and waited for his change, the boy with the tear-stained face walked past. The phone booth now stood empty.

Nick dialed the operator, and gave her Kate's number. He was calling collect. He heard Kate's "Hello?" His heart beat fast. The operator was asking Kate if she would accept a collect call from Nick Stampano. There was a long pause. As he waited, Nick pulled at the pan-flute in his jacket pocket. It was stuck.

"All right," came Kate's reply, "I'll take the call."

Nick yanked the flute from his pocket. He cradled the phone between his ear and his shoulder. He needed both hands to play the flute. He set his lips to the reeds, and began playing a sweet, sad melody. He put his heart into it. Through the music he was telling her that he was sorry, and that he loved her. "Surely we are meant to be together," the music pleaded.

The notes from the pan-flute filled the phone booth and floated out to the sidewalk. A small tree nearby seemed almost to be listening. Its roots grew under the sidewalk, but the sweet notes drifted through its bare, cold branches.

Nick lifted his mouth from the flute. With his ear still squeezed to the phone, he listened. "Kate? Are you there?" There was only a dial tone. She'd hung up.

"When is Nick coming back?" Glen waited for Hank to stop hammering at his table and answer. The church bells up on 7th Avenue were ringing again. They were calling to Glen. He couldn't wait any longer. It was now or never.

"Hank, I hate to leave you here alone, but I..."

Hank waved him away with the hammer. "Go on, get out of here. You're making me nervous."

"You sure?"

At the curb, Glen decided to act like a New Yorker and not wait for the green light. But halfway across Greenwich—"Holy Cow!"—he had to leap to the curb as a truck barely missed him.

Glen was headed for the large stone church, up a block on 7th Avenue. When he'd first heard the bells ringing that morning, an idea had popped into his head. Why hadn't he thought of it before?

Reaching the church, he paused below the wide stone steps leading up to the entrance. Above, the two huge doors were flung open, the service was over. Glen began climbing the steps and met with streams of people coming down. He was fighting his way upstream, like the salmon in the creeks back home. By the time he reached the top, he was out of breath. He paused for a moment, huffing and puffing. If he could lose these last 20 or 30 pounds, everything would be different. He'd start lifting weights to build muscle. He'd have a flat stomach for the first time since he was 10.

Inside the empty church, Glen pulled off his Christmas hat. The light was dim. He ran his hand back through his short brown hair. He realized he was sweating. And it was warm here, in this vast, hollow space.

He paused to bend a knee and cross himself, before walking towards the front. His steps echoed. A bank of candles flickered to the left of the altar. Glen kneeled down at the rail. He was still sweating. Maybe it wasn't just from the climb up the stairs. Maybe he was nervous at what he was about to do.

Not all of the candles were lit yet. To light a candle was to send your prayer to heaven.

Glen slipped a dollar bill into the collection box. Then he lit a fresh candle. The light reflected in his eyes. He closed them, pursed his lips together, and bowed his head.

He was 40 years old. He lived alone in a trailer. Four nights a week he made pizza in his cafe and delivered it around the village in his truck. The other three nights of the week he played cards, visited friends, or read books on naval warfare. He had studied every major sea battle of the Second World War. He knew the names of every ship and its commander.

Head bowed, Glen clasped his hands together on the rail. What he didn't know was all the names of the saints. But he knew that Saint Jude helped women to find husbands. Maybe the Saint could send one of those nice women his way. Silently, Glen prayed:

"Saint Jude, I need your help. I've never been married. I've been waiting for the right woman to come along. I know I'm a little overweight. But I've seen other guys, fatter than me, even right here in New York City, they're walking down the street with a woman on their arm."

At that moment someone knelt down at the rail beside him. He could smell a wonderful perfume. He could hear the person breathing. The perfume smelled like wildflowers. A thought raced through Glen's head: *Maybe my prayer has already been answered. Maybe this is the one.*

He kept his head bowed, but opened his eyes to slits and peered sideways. It was a woman, an elderly woman wearing a flowered scarf. Her eyes were closed, her lips moving in prayer.

Back at the hut, Hank had run out of nails. The table still needed one more leg. He came out from the little shelter and looked up and down the sidewalk. No sign of Glen or Nick. He only needed four more nails.

"Oops, sorry," said Hank, and stepped back. He'd been blocking the sidewalk. There were lots of people hurrying past.

So this was New York. All his life he'd heard about New York City, and about Greenwich Village. Greenwich Village was where all the creative people hung out—actors, dancers, writers.

Hank sighed. His first day in New York, and he was already homesick. He pulled his jackknife from his pocket and opened its blade. Picking up a stub of two-by-four, he squatted down, and began to whittle. Shavings of wood curled off and fell to the sidewalk.

Hank couldn't help it. His spirits were low. He squatted there in front of the hut, a small man dressed in red socks, green knickers and red suspenders. His knife bit into the wood.

"What are you doing?" asked a small voice.

Hank looked up. A little girl stood before him. She wore fur earmuffs and a coat with a fur collar. An older boy held her by the hand. The boy was tugging her to come along. "Wait, Bubba. I want to see what Santa's elf is doing." She peered again at the small knife in Hank's hand, and at the carved stick of wood. "What are you making?"

Hank's smile spread beneath his handlebar mustache. "What would you like me to make?"

The child shrugged. She looked up at her brother for help. He only tried to pull her away. "Wait!" she cried. To Hank she said, "I sent my list to Santa already of what I want. I'm not supposed to be greedy." But she eyed the stick, as if it might hold something wonderful.

Her brother pulled her away. "Bye," she waved. "Tell Santa I am being good."

Hank watched them go. His heart ached in his chest. He already missed his own little daughter, Celia.

His sad thoughts were suddenly shattered by the blast of a truck horn. Another long blast sounded as someone leaned on his horn. Then came a shout, "Anybody here?"

Hank folded his knife and jumped up. He squinted into the afternoon sun. A long flatbed truck had pulled up behind the van on the one-way street. That was legal. But it wasn't legal for the truck's rear end to stick out into the intersection. Cars on Greenwich Avenue were having to drive around.

A young kid in dark glasses climbed down from the cab of the truck. He couldn't have been more than 18. He was pulling on a pair of gloves. He paid no attention to the fact that his big truck was blocking traffic. He seemed not to hear all the horns honking angrily. He looked Hank up and down. "You the one who's gonna help me unload these trees?"

Hundreds of trees filled the truck's long deck. Row upon row of green firs lay on their sides. Each tree was tightly bound, its branches gathered close with twine. The whole load was secured with ropes. Already the kid in dark glasses was untying the knots. He'd pulled himself up onto the edge of the deck.

"Where are they from?" Hank shouted up. He didn't know what to do. The kid loosened a rope and tossed it to the sidewalk. "From Canada. The Fraser firs are from North Carolina. You gonna help, or just stand there?" He tossed a bundle of tiny trees down to Hank. "We call these little ones 'Charlie Browns.' "

Hank caught each bundle as it flew through the air. The fresh scent of the trees filled his senses. There was still snow on some of the trees. Snow got down his neck, the ice melting against his skin. His hands grew sticky with pitch from the trees. The kid up on the truck never stopped. Now he was tossing down the bigger firs. The stacks of wrapped trees along the sidewalk grew higher. Hank had no time to catch his breath.

But here came Nick and Glen to help.

"It's about time you guys showed up!" Hank gasped as he

caught an eight-foot balsam fir in his arms. "Where were you guys?"

Without a word, Nick climbed up to the deck of the truck. He grabbed a 12-footer from a pile at the back end. Seeing him, the kid straightened up. He had to yell over the honking horns of the traffic. "That pile is Douglas fir. Keep them separate from the rest!"

Nick tossed the Douglas fir down to Glen, who caught the big fir wrapped in twine. He laid it to one side, as well as the ones that followed. And here came a clear plastic sack filled with wreaths. There must have been 50 wreaths in the bag. Glen caught it, stumbled, but regained his balance.

The needles of the trees pricked their hands. The fragrant smell of the branches rubbed off on their clothes, as well as the pitch.

At last the kid in sunglasses climbed down from an empty deck. The load of 200 trees lay on the sidewalk. He pulled off his gloves.

Nick pointed up at the deck. "What about that?" The big yellow object looked like some kind of cement mixer.

"Oh yeah. That's the tree wrapper. I'll get it." And he swung himself up onto the deck again. The barrel of the tree wrapper was shaped like a cone, smaller at one end. The kid lowered it down with Nick's help. "And this is to cover the Douglas fir when it rains." He tossed down a tarp. "After harvest the Douglas fir lose their needles if they get wet."

Hank drew in a deep breath, breathing in the fragrance of the firs all around them. "It smells like home."

Nick slowly nodded. "Yeah..."

The kid jumped down from the flatbed. "I'll bring you some tree stands with the next batch of trees."

"More trees?" Glen glanced around at the 200 trees lying on the sidewalk. "When will that be?"

"In three days. I'll deliver late at night, when there's not so much traffic. This batch is just to get you started. Oh, and here's the price list." The kid glanced around at the three men. "No offense, but aren't you guys kind of old to be doing this?"

Nick laughed low in his throat. "Say," he lifted his chin. "How old are you?"

"Almost 19."

Smiling, Nick pushed up the fringed sleeves of his jacket. "What would you say to having an arm wrestle, you and me? I got me a punching bag at home, keeps me in shape."

The kid tilted his dark glasses to the top of his head. His eyes narrowed, wary.

"Come on." Nick shrugged. "Just for fun." He held up his right hand, with its strong wrist.

The kid looked at him, at this small, grey-haired man with his dark shining eyes. Then he shook his head, with a half smile. "No way."

Nick laughed, a husky sound. "In that case, let's shake hands." And he pressed his other hand over the top of their joined hands. "Hey, Merry Christmas, eh?"

Mr. Baxter

Every day Mr. Baxter ate the same thing for lunch. He heated up a can of Campbell's tomato soup. To go with the soup, he grabbed a handful of Ritz crackers from the box.

He sat at the window as he ate, and looked down at the street. The worst part of living alone was eating alone. When he had worked, he and his partner had always eaten at the same little cafe. Mr. Baxter would greet the waitress, set his gun in its holster on the counter, and be served his usual ham and cheese sandwich. There would be a lot of laughing and joking.

And then, when he'd come home at night, his wife would have dinner waiting for him. Sometimes she would put candles on the table.

In his memory, the bright flames flickered, then blurred. But there was no use crying into his soup.

Across the avenue, the three strangers were busy setting up their business. One of the big firs was being untied. Freed from the twine, the branches sprang open. The tree was then leaned against the chain-link fence. Its crown reached all the way up to the barbed wire that ran along the top of the fence, 12 feet up. A giant of a tree.

Mr. Baxter hadn't brought a Christmas tree into the apartment in over 30 years. All Christmas ads arriving in the mail were quickly stuffed into the garbage can under the sink.

At that moment, another Christmas ad began playing on the TV to the music of "Silent Night." Mr. Baxter winced. But he left the TV on. He kept it turned low, the voices murmuring all day and all night. He never turned it off. He needed the sound of human voices.

3

Evening – Same Day

Darkness had fallen. It was Sunday night, and on the sidewalk a new forest had sprung up. Christmas trees of all sizes leaned along the chain-link fence.

And along the curb, a crude fence of two-by-fours had been erected. Trees leaned against this fence as well. People passing along the sidewalk walked through a moist and fragrant forest. They walked past a little hut in that forest. Green firs leaned against the sides of the hut. More trees leaned against the front, where wreaths hung all around a doorway. A faint light within shone through the branches. The sound of a flute drifted out the open doorway. The notes traced a sad, lonely flight. Nick's eyes were closed as he played. His high forehead gleamed in the light from a small lamp.

"You mean she just hung up on him?" asked Hank.

Glen nodded with a grimace.

The three men huddled around the little heater. They sat on their rolled-up sleeping bags. They had built the little shelter around the subway grate in the sidewalk. And now a braid of garlic hung from a post. Pictures from home had been tacked along the edge of a shelf. The fragrance of the balsam firs shut out the fumes of exhaust. Even the noise of the traffic was muffled by the trees surrounding the little hut.

The notes of the pan-flute died away. A subway train passed underground, and the roar rose from the grate with a whoosh of stale air.

"But what did you say to her, Nicki? You must have said something that made her mad."

Nick looked off to one side. "I didn't say nothing, man."

"One of us had better get out there and sell trees," muttered Hank. He rose to his feet. But then he just stood there, by his two friends. It was cold outside. In fact it was cold inside as well, but not *as* cold. The little heater was like a campfire that they'd gathered around. Its wires hummed with a reddish glow. The glow held Hank in a kind of trance. It was hard to turn away. Maybe he'd just stand in the doorway, in case anyone came by for a Christmas tree.

Hank turned to confront a short, black-haired man wearing a black-and-white checked jacket. The man had his hands in his jacket pockets, with his fingers pointing forward like two guns. He took a step forward. Hank took a step back. Maybe they *were* guns.

Hank stared, wide-eyed.

The man's face was unshaven, with two days' dark growth on the cheeks. His eyes bulged, they seemed about to pop. Instead, a wild laugh burst from his mouth. He laughed with his mouth wide open. Hank took another step back.

The man gasped for breath, and glanced over his shoulder, "I had him going, didn't I?" And another loud laugh brayed forth. He took his gloved hand from his pocket and wiped his mouth. Then he held out his gloved hand.

Hank looked down at it with distaste.

"Just a little spit!" But the man drew off his glove. His face was now sober. His voice was flat when he spoke. "I'm your boss. Name's Mitch Hammer. You can call me Hammer. Everybody does. They know I don't take any crap. The old Hammer—that's me with the ladies. I give 'em a good pounding." He made obscene movements with his hips. His laugh was chill.

Hank had the feeling that was the last laugh they would hear from Mr. Hammer. His hand felt like it was caught in a vise. Mr. Hammer hadn't let go yet. Instead, he jerked his head over his shoulder. "This is my son. He's driving me around today. I'm teaching him to drive."

The tall gangly boy was standing just outside the doorway. His face was spotted with pimples, but he towered over his father. Mr. Hammer now glanced around the hut. "Looks like you've taken good care of yourselves here." He looked directly at Hank. "Now how about getting down to business." He let go of Hank's hand. "You come out to the car."

Hank rubbed his sore hand. "I'm not really the one to—"

But the boss had already turned on his heel, expecting Hank to follow.

Hank tugged nervously on his mustache. At that moment Nick laid a hand on his shoulder. "Relax, man," came the whisper. "Don't let him scare you, we're comin' too. These guys talk big, but they all had mothers." He nudged Hank toward the doorway.

But Mr. Hammer had stopped right outside the hut. He now waved his arms. "It's too dark here. You got all these trees. Nobody is gonna walk through here. They'll be afraid of being mugged." He turned to face his son. "Right?"

Mr. Hammer didn't wait for an answer. He continued talking to Hank. "Tomorrow, you guys go out and buy light bulbs. A bunch of light bulbs and some cord. You hang a string of light bulbs, 25 feet that direction..." He turned. "And 25 feet that direction." He called over his shoulder to his son, "Go get a string of coloured lights from the station wagon. Go on, move. In fact, bring two strings. And the boom box. *Move!*"

A well-dressed couple walked by. A large German shepherd dog trotted ahead of them on a leash.

Mr. Hammer watched them pass. In a coarse whisper he asked, "What do you think? You think she does it with the dog?"

Glen cleared his throat. "Sir..."

" 'Sir.' I like the sound of that."

"Sir, I noticed that the van doesn't have a license plate. I'd sure hate us to get in trouble over that."

He was ignored. Hammer was again addressing Hank. "These strings of lights... Put them on one of your biggest trees, one of the 12-footers. The customers walk by, they see your display tree all lit up, they want one just like it." He took the boom box from his son. "And be sure to keep Christmas carols playing on this."

Then he crooked his finger at Glen. "Come with me."

There was a beat-up station wagon parked in front of the van. From the back of the wagon the boss lifted out a stack of license plates. He shuffled through them. There must have been at least 10 of the metal plates. "Here. Here's your goddamn license."

"Sir, one other thing. I was wondering…"

"Well, don't." The back window of the station wagon slammed down. The gangly teenager was already sitting up front in the driver's seat. Mr. Hammer walked around to the passenger door. He paid no attention to the traffic whizzing by, a foot away.

By now, Hank and Nick had joined Glen at the curb.

The boss swung open the passenger door. A taxicab swerved, honking. He ignored it. Instead he called back to the trio. "And don't go telling anybody you're Canadians."

"You mean it's illegal for us to do this?" cried Glen.

"Just keep your mouth shut," yelled the Boss. "And keep your eyes to yourself. If you see something happen—well, you don't see it." Then he repeated himself, loudly but slowly, as if speaking to a group of children. "If you see something… you don't see it. That's how you stay out of trouble in New York."

"Wait," cried Glen in earnest from the curb. "Why did you hire us, if we're not supposed to be here working?"

Hammer decided to ignore him once again. Instead he addressed Hank. "From now on, you see this station wagon drive up, come over to the window. You hand in the cash from the day before. I got 50 Christmas tree lots just like this one, all over the city. I won't have time to stop and chat with all you Canadians. You understand?"

He ducked into the car.

Then he stood up again. "I'll tell you why I hire Canadians. No New Yorker would be willing to live on the street for a month in the middle of the goddamn winter."

The door slammed. The station wagon lurched forward, jerking, then picked up speed down 7th Avenue.

Glen watched the boss and his son depart. "I wanted to ask him if we need a license to sell Christmas trees. He didn't give me a chance."

"He's a creep," muttered Hank.

Nick was silent. He shook his head. When he finally spoke, his voice was husky. "I just keep doing my deep breathing. No sense taking in the energy of this guy." He turned his head in the opposite direction. The street lamp lit his craggy profile. "Relax Glennie. We don't need any license to sell trees. I checked it out. The city passed a law, long time ago."

Out on 7th Avenue, streetlights shone down on the Sunday night traffic. Steam escaped from manhole covers in the pavement. The clouds of steam rose white in the headlights of the waiting traffic.

"Can someone tell me how much this tree is?" It was a woman's voice, from behind them. All three men turned towards the sound. She was on the other side of the Christmas trees, in front of their little shelter.

Hank called out, “Be right there!”

But Glen was faster. He squeezed through a gap in the fence. “Howdy do! You need some help, Miss? That one? Oh, that one is probably cheap.” He called to Nick. “How much would you say, Nick? Three bucks? Let’s say three bucks.” By the way, I’m Glen. And you’re…” He didn’t wait for the young woman to reply. “I hope you don’t think I’m being rude to ask your name. But I’m from Canada, you see. I’m not a New Yorker.” He paused to get his breath. He knew he was talking too much and too fast, but he couldn’t help it. Women made him nervous. And this was the most beautiful woman he’d ever seen. He leaned forward, his voice filled with concern. “You don’t think three bucks is too much?”

All this time the young woman had been studying the little tree. She stood it on the sidewalk and twirled it around in the dim light from the streetlamp. She wore a short black coat over black tights and high heeled boots. The tights showed off her legs. They were shapely with muscles, strong.

Glen set the boom box on the sidewalk. “You’ve caught us on our first day here. We’re going to string up lights, fix things up… Stop by anytime,” he added, as if she were already leaving. But she wasn’t.

She leaned the tree back among the others. She tossed the end of her long scarf over her shoulder. “So you guys are from Canada?”

Glen gulped, nodding. *She was talking to him. This beautiful woman was talking to him.*

"I've always wanted to see Canada." Her voice was wistful. She looked around at the firs and pines leaning everywhere. "This is like being in the woods, isn't it?"

Glen was still speechless.

"Oh, is this where you live?" She poked her head through the doorway of wreaths. In the dim light her face was pale. She had high cheekbones. In fact she looked bone thin—except for her muscular legs. To Glen she looked fragile.

"You must eat like a bird," he blurted.

"How much are these?" She was fingering one of the wreaths that framed the doorway.

Glen turned. "How much are the wreaths, Hank?"

Hank searched his pockets for the price list. "I've got it here somewhere..."

"Oh, don't bother. I'll be back. I come by here every night on my way home from rehearsal."

Hank's ears pricked up. "Rehearsal? Are you an actor?"

The young woman hitched up the strap of her big shoulder bag. "I'm a dancer. I'm with the New York City Ballet."

Glen whistled. "Holy cow! Let me shake your hand. Wow! I'm shaking the hand of a real live ballet dancer." His big paw had engulfed her small bony hand.

"Ouch."

"Oh jeez. Did I hurt you? I guess I don't know my own strength."

"No, it's not you." She rubbed her wrist. "I fell tonight. Actually, my partner dropped me."

"Dropped you?" squeaked Hank.

"Um-hum." She shivered, and hugged herself to keep warm. "I'd better get home. I haven't eaten all day."

"You haven't?" Glen checked his watch. "It's almost nine o'clock at night!"

"Oh, well, black coffee and half a bagel."

"*Half* a bagel? You're starving yourself!"

Nick had stepped from the hut. Now he held out a small wrinkled paper bag. He shook it, a dry rustle, and murmured to the dancer, "Go ahead, put your hand in. Go on. I dried them myself." The cloud of his breath hung in the cold air. He looked into her face. "What's your name?"

"Jennifer."

"Go on, Jennifer, try one."

Jennifer reached into the paper bag. She pulled out a small piece of dried fruit. It was brown and ugly.

"Now, I know that don't look like your dried pear at the supermarket. But you taste that. Yeah... sink your teeth into it. There's no sprays on that pear, no chemicals." Nick watched her face. "Good, huh?"

She nodded, chewing.

"Here, take a handful. To hold you over till your dinner."

Glen cut in. "You know, maybe it's not my place to say anything. But maybe you should be more careful, walking by yourself at night. I mean, we're nice guys—"

"I know, I saw you this morning when I walked to rehearsal." She swallowed the last of the dried pear.

Glen started in surprise. "You did? You walked right past here?"

"Um-hum." She smiled for the first time. "You three guys looked pretty lost. Anyway, you don't need to worry, I have protection." She patted her coat pocket.

Hank eyes widened. *A gun, she carries a gun.*

She bit into another dried pear, and began to chew. It took a lot of chewing. Finally she swallowed. "Thanks for these," she said to Nick. "They're delicious. But I'll just take three—no, four." And she dropped the rest back into his paper bag. "Goodnight," she called. The heels of her high boots clicked on the sidewalk.

"Toodledy-doo," Glen waved.

Hank stood beside him, watching her go. "I can't believe it. She carries a gun in her pocket." There was awe in his voice.

"Maybe it was just a can of pepper spray."

"Oh!" Hank slapped the pocket of his knickers. "I forgot. I found the price list." He drew out the piece of paper and unfolded it. He ran his finger down the list, then gave a low whistle. "Glen, that wasn't a three-dollar tree she was looking at. We're supposed to sell that size for $25."

"But that's robbery!"

Someone was shaking Hank's shoulder. He was being rocked back and forth. Someone was rocking him, and saying something. In his dream, Hank was out in the rowboat, on the lake. The lake was rocking. Someone's hand was on his shoulder, calling his name.

"Hank, wake up. You gotta get up now..."

Hank pushed the hand off his shoulder. He had to row. It was cold on the lake. He was rowing out from shore. Little Celia stood on the shore. She was waving. "Daddy!" she cried, "Take me with you. I want to come too!"

"Hank, you gotta wake up. I got some hot coffee here for you. Yeah, man, sit up, that's it."

"What time is it?"

"It's three o'clock in the morning. It's time for your shift. I gotta get some sleep myself."

Hank crawled slowly from his sleeping bag. Then he lifted its warmth around his shoulders, and crawled past Glen. Glen's snoring had kept Hank awake for much of the night. And there'd been all those sirens screaming past on the street.

Hank climbed out of the van and into the little hut. He stood swaying, with the sleeping bag around his shoulders. He'd slept in his clothes.

"Hey, here's the coffee I got you." Nick handed him a paper cup. "And here's a donut to go with it. It's day-old. The baker down on Greenwich gave me a bag for free. He gets up at two in the morning to start work. Can you believe that?"

Hank stood on the subway grate in front of the little heater. He sipped the hot coffee. He had to keep his eyes open. Maybe he should try walking.

Outside on the sidewalk he paced slowly back and forth among the Christmas trees. He took a bite of donut. The dream about his little daughter was still with him. He missed her. *Maybe this is how mothers feel.* Of course, Celia was safe. He didn't have to worry. She was staying at her mother's house for the month of December. "Celia's safe," Hank repeated to himself. He'd reached the end of the Christmas trees, where an alley cut across the sidewalk. There he stopped to turn around.

He could hear music, faintly. Jazz music, being played over at the Village Vanguard. The notes floated across 7th Avenue. A few cars still sped past. But since it was three o'clock in the morning, they were mostly taxicabs.

Taxicabs for people too drunk to drive home, mused Hank. He stood there for a while, listening to the music drifting over. There was a long black limousine parked in front of the club.

Hank let his gaze wander up the side of the building directly across 7th Avenue. There he noticed a square of blue, flickering light. The blue square was a window, showing the flickering light of a TV within. It was on the third floor. *Amazing. That old guy is still awake.*

Hank was freezing. Maybe he'd better keep walking. He took another sip of coffee, and a bite of donut. He chuckled to himself. *I'm a night watchman in the middle of eight million sleeping people.*

The donut was gone by the time he'd reached the other end of the Christmas tree lot. He wiped the crumbs from his mustache. Standing at the corner, he sipped the last of the coffee. He was wide-awake now.

A garbage truck rumbled down Greenwich and stopped. There

were piles of refuse set out along the curbs for pick up. But there was more than just garbage in these piles. Hank walked a little ways down Greenwich. He picked up an umbrella from a pile. He opened it, closed it. It was a perfectly good umbrella, with only one strut broken. He tucked it under his arm and strolled on. He found a frying pan, and a cup with a broken handle.

All the while, the garbage truck beeped a warning signal. *Beep Beep Beep* it warned as it backed up to each pile. *Beep Beep Beep,* meaning "Danger, Look out."

Hank's heart jumped as he spied a chair on one of the piles. It was a dainty wooden chair. The back was carved. Its velvet seat had a small rip in the cloth. It was the kind of a chair that a lady would keep in her bedroom. Hank guessed the dark wood to be walnut. *Beep Beep Beep.* The garbage truck was backing up to the pile with the chair on top.

Hank wanted that chair. But something was pulling him in the opposite direction. He had a strong feeling that he should go back to the Christmas tree lot. *Beep Beep Beep*. Hank set down the treasures that he'd rescued and ran back, holding the sleeping bag around his shoulders. As he rounded the corner, he saw a shadowy figure. It was a man, a big man. He had just lifted one of the larger firs to his shoulder.

"Hey!" Hank shouted, and stopped short.

Hank didn't pause to think. A small man, he rose to his tiptoes. He lifted the sleeping bag from his shoulders and spread it wide above his head. He became seven feet tall. "Hi-hi-hi!" he screeched. This was the way to bluff a bear. You puffed yourself up big and yelled sharp noises. "Hi-hi-hi!" Of course, that's what you do if it's a black bear. But if the bear is a grizzly, you make yourself small. Maybe this was a grizzly…

But no. The big man dropped the tree and took off running down 7th Avenue.

Beep Beep Beep.

Hank tossed the sleeping bag into the hut and ran back around the corner. He ran across Greenwich. The garbageman had lifted up the little chair. He was about to throw it into the garbage truck's grinding jaws.

"Stop!" Hank ran up and grabbed the chair. "I'll take it," he gasped. Then he ran back across the street, where he picked up the rest of his treasures.

Back at the hut, he set the little walnut chair in the doorway and sat down. He braced his hands on his knees. He was panting and his heart pounded. He hadn't even had time yet to be afraid. But now he had time. What a fool! He'd put himself in danger for an $80 tree!

Finally Hank's breathing eased, his heart calmed, and he could smile at what he'd done. He even laughed aloud. "This is the weirdest camping trip I've ever been on."

The heater warmed his back from inside the hut. Hank leaned down and picked up a stick of wood. He decided to whittle to pass the time. He reached in the pocket of his knickers for his jackknife.

Just then, a yellow cab pulled into the alley down 7th. The back door of the cab opened slowly. It was easy to see that the passenger getting out was drunk. He held onto the cab door to steady himself. "Wait here," he called loudly to the cab driver. His voice was slurred.

Hank stood up from the little chair. His hand was still in his pocket, with his fingers curled around the knife. The man lurched towards him. "Is thish a place sells trees?"

Hank drew his hand from his pocket, without the knife. "You bet. How can I help you?" He grabbed the man's elbow to keep him from falling.

"Need a tree." The drunk man lifted his hand above his head. "Tall tree." Then he drew out his wallet. He began pulling out bills. He swayed on his feet. "My wife, she won't be mad if I bring home a tree."

"Is this one tall enough?" Hank bent down for the fir that the thief had dropped to the sidewalk. He stood it upright.

The man nodded, without looking at the tree. He was trying to count the bills in his hands. "How much?" he muttered, swaying. "How much money you want?"

"Eighty dollars." Hank had pushed the fir into the barrel of the tree wrapper. He now walked around to the other end, where there was a hole two feet across. He slid a ring of plastic netting around the rim of the hole. Then he gripped the butt end of the tree and began pulling it through the barrel. The fir's branches were pressed up around its trunk. Hank pulled out the tree. It was now a tall slim column of branches wrapped with green plastic netting.

The drunk man held out a spread of $20 bills. "Here, take it all."

"I can't do that." Hank took the money, picked out four 20's, and handed back the rest. The drunk lurched, grabbing at Hank's shoulder for support.

There was a little trouble getting him back into his cab. And then he wanted the Christmas tree to lie across his lap.

The cabbie jumped out. "That tree's not ridin' in here."

So the taxi drove off down 7th Avenue with a beautiful balsam fir slanting from its trunk.

Hank was left standing in the middle of the alley. For the moment, no siren wailed, no horn honked. And the garbage truck had rumbled on. The odd car or taxi sped by on 7th. For the moment, Hank appeared to be the only person on the street.

What was that sound? He tilted his head, to hear better. It sounded like an owl had just hooted.

The long black limousine was still parked across the broad avenue. The limo had those darkly-tinted windows that hid its passengers from curious eyes. A white cloud of exhaust snaked from the tailpipe. The motor was running.

There it was again! *Whoo… whoo*. A faint quaver, like an owl calling in the forest. How could there be an owl in the city? He must be hearing things. He probably had jet lag.

Whoo… whoo…

But it wasn't the hoot of an owl. It was a voice—a faint, human voice, and it quavered with fear.

A chill ran down Hank's spine. He was trembling with cold. He should go get his sleeping bag and put it around his shoulders. But he didn't move. His gaze was fixed on the black limo. The sound was coming from over there.

Slowly the limo had started to move, so slowly. Was it moving? Hank couldn't really tell. *Yes*. By inches it slowly moved south and revealed the figures of two men. One of the men faced the wall of the brick building. His hands were above his head, with the fingers spread out as if to cling to the bricks for support. His head was turned to one side, his cheek pressed to the wall. *Whoo...* The faint call of an owl, hooting in the forest's dark night. *Whoo... whoo*. The barrel of a gun was being held to his temple. A muffled thud sounded, and the man's fingers slid down the bricks. He crumpled to a heap on the sidewalk.

The far door of the limo slammed shut as the long black car continued to move along the curb. Then it moved out onto 7th Avenue. Hank could barely hear the rich purr of its motor. The limousine simply slipped away. Under every streetlight its sleek black form appeared again, then disappeared until the next streetlight. Hank watched until it finally became merely a glint of light among other lights.

He couldn't bear to turn his head back. Had he really seen what he had seen? He felt nothing. His mind was a blank.

Slowly he turned his head—ever so slowly.

A burst of laughter made him jump. Five men were coming out of the jazz club. More peals of laughter rang out—hollow in that early-morning hour. The five men all carried instrument cases. Musicians. Three of the men were black, and older. Their laughter rang out with a deep bass.

Then it stopped. They'd seen the man slumped by the wall.

One of the younger musicians walked slowly over to the crumpled heap. He nudged it with the toe of his shoe, then jumped back. "Shit!"

"What's the deal here?" One of the older men approached, and got down on one knee.

A blue square of light flickered in the corner of Hank's eye. He didn't move. Only his eyes moved up to the right. His gaze traveled up above that strange sign, "With Pain, or Without Pain." The old man was standing in the window looking down. Was he using binoculars again? He was only a dark form against the blue flickering light. But it seemed to Hank that the old guy was looking directly down at him.

Breathe, Hank told himself. He took a single step back towards the hut and the brown van. *Home*. Another step. His legs seemed about to buckle under him. Thoughts flashed through his mind. Voices too. But his mind remained a blank. He drew the little walnut chair into the hut. Voices flitted in his ear. His daughter's voice. The voice of that drunk.

Hank sat down on the chair's torn velvet seat. He drew his sleeping bag around his shoulders. He stared blankly at the red-hot wires of the heater. Subway trains passed below with a noisy clatter. Hank hardly noticed them. The one voice that lingered was the voice of the boss: "If you see something, you don't see it. If you see something, you don't see it."

Time passed. Outside, by 6:30 a.m., the traffic began to swell towards rush hour. The noise grew and grew. Horns blared. And now the wail of sirens stirred the city. People began passing by the hut's doorway. They were walking their dogs, or walking to work. Behind the chain-link fence, men opened the gate into the vacant lot. The crew loaded coils of plastic pipe onto a city maintenance truck.

At 8:10 a.m. Glen staggered out of the brown van. His hair was sticking up every which way and he needed a shave. Checking his watch, he looked at Hank, who sat hunched on a little chair in front of the heater.

"Hank! Your shift is over. Why didn't you wake us up?"

Hank remained silent. He only stared at the glowing heater, as if its warmth was the only thing that mattered in all the world.

Mr. Baxter

Mr. Baxter dialed the number of the local station house. He felt a tweak of pride that he still remembered the number. His binoculars hung on a heavy cord from his neck.

The phone rang and rang at the other end of the line. Of course it was the middle of the night, but someone was certain to be on duty.

Mr. Baxter would often study faces on the street with his binoculars. He would focus on someone standing below at the corner of 7th. The person might be waiting for the green light. Through the binoculars, Mr. Baxter would read the person's face, and judge his or her character.

Mr. Baxter had studied faces all his working life. He'd always prided himself on knowing human nature. You watch the eyes, the mouth. Under questioning, suspects can keep their eyes blank and dead-looking. But a twitch of the mouth will suddenly give them away.

The phone was still ringing. Finally someone answered, but they put him on hold.

Yes, his fellow policemen had always said that he was a good judge of character. But Mr. Baxter's wife had been of a different opinion. She had claimed that her husband never searched for the good in people. He was familiar with the lower aspects of human nature. But what about the higher aspects?

Mr. Baxter had never admitted that she was right. But of course, she was. Whenever his binoculars happened upon a face beaming with joy, Mr. Baxter shifted away. It was somehow embarrassing to peer into eyes shining with happiness. It was like trying to look into a too-bright light.

4

The 10th of December

Nick needed his coffee. It was hard to shave before having a cup of strong black coffee to wake him up.

He rinsed the razor blade under the faucet. Then he peered into the mirror again and pulled at his opposite cheek. He began to shave through the white foam. He'd been in New York for more than a week now. Things were going good. He had a routine. Shave first, then coffee.

Nick had already washed his hair and toweled it dry. His grey frizzy hair was now tamed into two short braids. Strips of black cloth hung down from each braid, making them appear longer. He ducked his head to the sink and rinsed off the last of the shaving cream.

Pressing the towel against his face, Nick said the word aloud: "Ad-ven-ti-tious."

It was his new word for the day. He'd been saying it over and over in his mind. With dry hands he reached into the pocket of his fringed jacket. He pulled out the little dictionary. He read the word's meaning again. "Adventitious: Something that comes to a man by mere luck, or from a stranger."

The door to the washroom banged open. A man in a wheelchair rolled in. He looked Nick up and down. Then he scowled, as if to say, "What are you doing here?"

Nick held up his hand, "Peace, man." He gathered up his shaving kit and towel and slipped out the bathroom door. It was a door marked "Handicapped Only." Nick liked to keep clean, and this was the cleanest washroom in Saint Vincent's Hospital.

In the hallway he nodded with respect towards a small statue of Saint Vincent. "How ya doing?" It was "Saint Vinny" to people in the neighbourhood.

Saint Vincent's Hospital was only a block away from the Christmas tree lot. Ambulance sirens howled day and night in this neighbourhood. But a person can get used to anything. Anything. Especially when they're in love, and there's hope.

Out on the street, the rain had stopped. The sidewalk shone wet in the pale sunshine. Nick dodged people along the crowded sidewalk. It seemed as if everyone was in a hurry except him. He strode along with a spring in his step. He hadn't given up hope. "Ad-ven-ti-tious," he sang under his breath. Kate was coming back to him, he knew it. He knew it right here—and his fist struck his chest. Wasn't there a Frank Sinatra song… "In my heart, you…"

"Hey! You can't come in here."

"Whadda you mean?" Nick stood in the doorway of Harry's Deli. "This is Nicki, your friend, I come in here every day."

"Not with bare feet, you don't. You step on something, get your feet cut, I get sued."

"Come on, Harry. Just grind me a handful of beans. I'll wait right here by the door." The delicious aroma of roasting coffee filled the Deli. Behind the counter, Harry grumbled. "Why do you bother me every morning? Why can't you buy a pound of coffee, even half a pound, like everybody else?"

"It's gotta be fresh ground, right? Come on, smile. Hey, it's a beautiful day out there."

It's gonna happen. Kate is coming back to me. Nick whistled tunelessly as he waited at the door. "That's French Roast, right? And a few Mexican beans?"

Nick walked out of Harry's Deli with the bag of coffee. He crossed Greenwich, still whistling. The rain had cleaned the city's dirty air. It smelled fresh. And the Christmas tree lot smelled like a forest smells after a storm—moist and fragrant. Christmas carols floated out from the boom box. Coloured lights twinkled on the huge balsam fir. They winked red, blue, green, yellow.

Steam rose from the wet trees as the sun shone down. Many of the trees now stood upright in blue metal stands. But most still leaned against the chain-link fence. Or they leaned against the homemade fence of two-by-fours along the curb.

Hank was pushing a broom down the centre of the sidewalk. He was sweeping up the needles fallen from the trees. A long white scarf hung from his neck. On his hands he wore short-fingered gloves. He pushed the broom halfheartedly. He moved as if the troubles of the world weighed on his narrow shoulders.

Nick called to him. "Hey, I saw that rat again last night."

Hank stopped sweeping. "How do you know it's the same rat?"

Nick thought for a moment. He pictured the tiny face with its quivering whiskers and beady black eyes. He nodded. "I know, yeah." And he went inside the little hut.

First he lit the campstove and poured water into the kettle from a plastic jug. Then he checked to see if his high moccasins were dry yet. It had rained for three days straight—a cold hard rain.

Nick had to admit that his bare feet were feeling the cold. He stepped over to the rug. The rug came from the dumpster down on Greenwich. It covered the subway grate, and muffled the noise and stale dirty air that blew up.

The water bubbled to a boil, and he threw in a pinch of coffee. "Hank?" he called from the doorway. "You think Kate got our letter yet?"

Hank set the broom aside. "It wasn't 'our' letter, Nick. It was your letter. You told me what to say. I just wrote it down for you."

"Yeah, but you spelled the words right. You made me look good."

"You *are* good, Nick. Kate knows that already."

"Well, what did we say?"

"*You* said that you were crazy about her, and that if she wanted this new guy, then that was okay. But that you were keeping her in your heart, just in case." Hank's gaze wandered down 7th Avenue.

There was a frown line between his brows. "And you described the neighbourhood, what goes on here."

"You think I'm a fool, Hank, right?"

"No, Nick. I don't think you're a fool." Hank spoke in a pained voice. "A fool is someone who fails to do what he knows in his heart is right."

"In my heart, man, in my heart..." Nick took a deep breath. "Oh yes, smell that coffee." Then he cocked his head, squinting at his friend. "Hank, let me ask you something. You feeling sick? 'Cause if you're sick, I can make you some tea instead of this coffee. I got some dried mint from home. Just say the word."

"Coffee's fine."

Nick lowered his voice to a husky whisper. "Hank, you been like this for days. What's goin' on? You never have a laugh, or play music. Where's your concertina? I thought you brought your concertina along."

"It's still in my pack." Hank turned his head away. "I just don't feel like playing."

"No, I'm serious here. Is the city getting you down? You homesick?"

Tears sprang to Hank's eyes. He kept his head turned away. "I can't leave now. I need the money."

Nick nodded. "Yeah, we all need the money. Hey, you know, I saw that beggar again with the crutch, shaking his tomato can." Nick pursed his lips. "He got another buck out of me. Yeah... I dunno about him." A smile crept to Nick's mouth. "With what I earn this month, I'm gonna fix up my house, build a bathroom onto one side. Kate, she don't like using the outhouse when she visits from Calgary." Nick's smile widened. "Yeah," he murmured, "She's comin' back to me." He started whistling. He pinched off a clove of garlic from the braid. "I'm gotta start my sauce. It's gotta cook all day."

Hank moved outside with his coffee cup. It was the cup with the broken handle. The cup that he'd found that terrible night more than a week ago.

Some of the people walking past smiled at him, and Hank did his best to smile back. He was relieved when he saw a bulldog trotting down the sidewalk. At least he wouldn't have to pretend to be cheerful.

The bulldog was straining towards him on a leash.

"Hello, Lucky." Hank squatted down. The bulldog wore a small coat fastened with silver buttons along his back. "Good dog. Give Uncle Hank a kiss." A wide, hot tongue lapped at Hank's nose.

The man holding the leash giggled. "Do I get a kiss from Uncle Hank too?"

Hank looked up at the dog's owner. "Did you remember to put sugar in the water for your Christmas tree?" Hank waited, then became impatient. "You know, in the stand."

"Sugar? Nick said to add a tablespoon of bleach."

Hank rubbed Lucky's ears. "Sugar, bleach. Either one will help the tree keep its needles." Hank could hear the flatness in his own voice. Something had gone out of him. He'd lost his faith. "Good dog, Lucky." *My faith in what? In life? In my fellow man? Perhaps it's just that I've lost faith in myself.*

That's why people love dogs. They don't judge you. They greet you as if you were still a wonderful person. For a moment, you feel that perhaps they're right. But only for a moment.

Hank stood up just in time, before Lucky could snatch the Canada hat off his head. But Lucky had snagged something else with his teeth. Hank's long white scarf slid slowly off his neck.

Then Lucky spied another dog. The tasty scarf was forgotten. He strained forward on his leash. The other dog was lifting his hind leg against a Scotch pine.

"Shoo! Scat!" Hank ran over, waving his arms. Dogs loved this new forest on the corner of 7th and Greenwich. There were so many trees to choose from.

Glen lent a hoarse yell. "Hey, get away from there!" He was coming across Greenwich carrying a bag of groceries. Whenever a dog paused in front of a Christmas tree to do his duty, the needles would turn yellow. "Did you stop him in time?" he called to Hank.

The two met in front of the hut. The hut's doorway was framed with wreaths. Christmas carols from the boom box sang out the old hopes, the old joys. Glen grimaced at Hank. "I was over in one of the hospital johns. No toilet paper. And there was blood everywhere."

Hank paled at the mention of blood.

Glen shrugged his big round shoulders. "But I shouldn't be surprised. After all, it's the bathroom in the Emergency Ward." He looked down at the bag of groceries in his arms. "I better take these in to Nick. I can smell garlic frying."

Hank picked up the broom again and started pushing it slowly along the sidewalk. He made a second sweep past the hut. That's when he overheard Nick ask Glen, "You got the tomato paste?"

"It's right there in the bag with the onions. Hand me the newspaper, will you? I want to see if they've solved the murder yet."

"What murder?" Nick must have been frying more garlic. Hank could smell the aroma.

"What murder?" Glen's voice sounded shocked. "I'm talking about the murder across the street, in front of that jazz club. Here it is," cried Glen from inside." 'Death at Village Vanguard.' "

Hank's heart pounded. He stood gripping the handle of the broom. Inside the hut, Glen was reading the newspaper article aloud. " 'Police offered no comment, when asked if the 34-year-old man shot in the early hours of December 2nd was affiliated with the Mafia.' "

Nick broke in. "What's that fancy word mean—'affiliated'?"

"It means 'belonged.' That the guy belonged to the Mafia."

"He did?"

"Wait—here it is. 'Police do admit to a lead in the shooting death of...' " Glen read on, "Yadda yadda yadda... Hey, listen to this. 'An eye witness has come forward. No arrests have been made at present.' "

Listening outside, Hank gasped. An eye witness! But he was the only eye witness. It had happened between 3:00 and 4:00 a.m., and there'd been no one else on the street!

Hank saw Jennifer coming towards him down the sidewalk. Quickly he bent to the broom again. From 10 feet away the dancer waved, and stepped from the stream of people walking to work.

She sniffed the air. "Mmm, what's cooking? What's that delicious smell? I could smell it a block away."

At the sound of Jennifer's voice, Glen stepped from the hut still holding open the newspaper. "Nick is cooking up his famous spaghetti sauce."

Every morning and evening, Jennifer passed through the Christmas tree lot. Every time, Glen greeted her with a flushed face. He now leaned forward, his shoulders hunched. "Are you on your way to rehearsal?"

"Um-hum." This was spoken over her shoulder, for she now leaned into the doorway of the hut.

"Jennifer. How ya doin'?" Nick grinned, but tears filled his eyes. He'd been chopping onions. He scooped up the diced pieces and threw them into the pan. "Say, why don't you stop by on your way home tonight—try my sauce." He shook the pan by its handle. The garlic and onion sizzled in the oil. "It's my mother's recipe. It's the best." He kissed the tips of his fingers.

Glen had crowded in behind Jennifer. He fingered a long pink ribbon hanging from her shoulder bag. "What's this?"

Jennifer lifted out a pink satin toe shoe. "I wear out a pair of these every week. This pair is almost ready for the trash." Two long ribbons hung from the shoe, but the shoe's satin was scuffed and dirty. The leather sole was worn and cracked under the arch.

Glen looked at the shoe with longing and burst out, "You can't throw them away!" Then he reddened, and stumbled over his words. "We'll hang them up on this nail—right, Nick? And I'll take them home, so my friends will believe me when I tell them I met a real ballerina."

Hank poked his head in. "Could somebody help me out here? We've got two customers."

"I'll go." Nick quickly poured a can of tomatoes into the pan. He turned the flame down to a simmer. He wiped his hands on his pants and stepped outside. "Anybody seen my gloves?" he asked of no one in particular. He approached a customer. The well-dressed man was stick-thin. His face was gaunt. There were open sores spotting his cheeks and forehead. He wasn't old. He couldn't have been over 35. But he looked tired, very tired. Nick greeted him with concern in his dark eyes. "I'm here to help you, man. Just ask. Whatever you want."

A wry smile creased the man's face. He spoke flatly. "Well, I'd like to live forever. Can you help me with that?"

Nick laughed, a low husky laugh. "My man, you have come to the right place. I'll tell you the answer in one word: garlic. I eat four, five cloves of garlic a day." Nick grinned. His smooth skin gleamed with health. "I grow garlic for a living, you see. I got a big patch of it, back home."

"Garlic..." The man smiled faintly at Nick's good nature, at his energy. And he seemed to draw some of that energy into himself. He drew a deep breath. "This is my last Christmas. I want the best, the biggest tree that you have for sale."

Nick cocked his head to one side. He didn't say anything for a moment. "Jingle Bells" was playing on the boom box.

Then he nodded. "Okay. Follow me. Over here we've got the

Rolls-Royce of Christmas trees." Nick lifted up an 11-foot fir, and shook out its branches. The tree towered above them both. People walking past brushed the swaying branches of the giant. "What you have here is a Fraser fir. Look at that colour. You can't exactly say it's blue... or green... or grey. You know what colour it looks to me?"

With a wry smile the man shook his head. He seemed amused by Nick.

"It looks the same colour as the coat of a wild wolf. A wolf with a bluish eye." Nick's own eyes lit up. "You believe me? Let me tell you, I know what I'm talking about. I used to own a wolf."

The man suddenly looked less tired. His voice lifted. "You did? You owned a wolf?"

"Well... truth? He was only half wolf. And I doubt he ever knew he was owned. I finally had to get rid of him."

The man appeared shocked. "You had him killed?"

"Killed? You crazy? I gave him to a young hippie."

Holding the tree upright, Nick leaned to brush raindrops from the fir's branches. "These Fraser firs, they keep their needles the longest of any tree we got. You treat this one right, put bleach in his water, you'll have him way after the New Year."

"The new year," repeated the man. "Yes, well..." He looked up into the towering tree, at its branches spreading wide. "I'll take it. I'll take the wolf." He seemed close to tears. Then he cleared his throat, and spoke in a flat voice. He was suddenly all business. "Can you deliver it to my apartment?" The man dug out his wallet.

Nick stole a glance at his face and neck. He kept his voice low.

"Let me ask you something. You ever tried aloe vera on those sores?"

The man looked at Nick as if he were crazy, or maybe stupid. Then he laughed. It was a hollow laugh, hollow of any mirth. "No, I haven't tried aloe vera." He began counting out bills from his wallet. "But thanks for the advice."

A heavy *thump, thump, thump* sounded from the radio of a passing car. The music beat like a giant heart that faded as the car passed on.

Inside the hut, the passing *thump, thump* mixed with a Christmas carol from the boom box. Glen paid little notice to either. He had ears only for Jennifer. She stood in front of the campstove. Her large bag still hung from her shoulder. Slowly she stirred Nick's sauce with a fork. "I should get going."

"No, no," urged Glen. "Go on with what you were saying. I'm all ears, really. You have time. No problem. Go on, I'm listening." *Something was happening here!*

"Well, it's just that I've held off so long. For 12 years I've put dance first. Every day since I was 16, I've practiced for four or five hours. *Every day.*" She turned towards Glen, the fork in her hand. "And now I want a life of my own. I want to start a family." She looked down at the pan. "But I feel so torn. I don't want to quit dance, but I—" She glanced over at the doorway.

Glen could have strangled Nick for walking in at that moment.

"How's my sauce coming?" Nick took the fork from Jennifer. He began crushing the tomatoes in the pan, pressing down with the tines of the fork. "That customer just now... Did you see his face? He had big sores all over his cheeks and forehead." Nick shook his head, "Terrible."

Glen nodded, "Sores..." He tried to appear interested.

"Yeah, open sores. They were all over his face and down his neck. You know, now that I think of it..." He stared off for a moment. "I've seen a lotta guys around here with sores like that." Then he reached into the grocery bag and pulled out a sausage. With a knife he began slicing it. "It must have something to do with living in the city. Maybe it's the bad air. Or the water. The water here, it's not fit to drink."

"It's AIDS," said Jennifer, in a matter-of-fact voice. "Your man with the sores has developed full-blown AIDS." She checked her wristwatch. "Listen you guys, I have to go, I'll see you later."

"Tonight?" asked Glen. "I guess you'll be stopping by on your way home from rehearsal, right?"

Jennifer tossed her long hair over her shoulder as she hurried down the sidewalk. He called after her. "Promise you'll save those toe shoes for me? You won't throw them out?"

Turning, she walked backwards for a few paces. "I promise," she called, and flashed him a warm smile that took his breath away.

Glen waved good-bye. "Toodledy-doo."

All afternoon Glen was in high spirits. He wore his Christmas hat, with its earflaps. It seemed to him that the customers were smiling more than usual. Or was it just him?

He pulled back the cuff of his sweatshirt, to check the watch on his thick wrist. It would be hours before Jennifer passed this way again, on her way home from rehearsal. *Hours*. Surely she'd been just about to confess something important. Glen went over what she'd been saying, just before Nick barged in. She'd been talking about settling down, starting a family.

Even though it was a cold, crisp day, Glen began to sweat. He tugged at the collar of his sweatshirt. He needed to go take a shower at the YMCA. Hank was over there now. Glen pulled off the fleece hat. He ran a hand over his hair. Maybe he should get a haircut too. He wanted to look his best for Jennifer, just in case. *In case what?*

Glen put his Christmas hat back on. Then he sat down by the doorway. He sat on the little walnut chair that Hank had rescued from the garbage. Hank had asked him not to. ("Glen, you're just too darned heavy," Hank had said.) But Glen figured that if he sat carefully, what harm? Merry music jingled from the boom box. "Only 14 more shopping days till Christmas, folks!"

The sun shone down with its feeble winter light. The streets and sidewalks were mostly dry now. But in the shade of tall buildings, the sidewalks had turned icy. Down on Greenwich Avenue, the grammar school had let out for the day. Children rushed along the sidewalks, pushing and shoving each other. Flocks of them passed by the hut on their way home. Some paused, banging their lunch boxes against their legs. They stared at Glen in his Christmas hat, sitting in front of the little Hobbit hut. Then they ran off. Glen smiled at them all, holding up his hand and giving a little wave, "Merry Christmas… Merry Christmas."

Why had Jennifer said what she'd said, about settling down? And why to him? Sure, they were friends. She always stopped by to say hello. But so did a lot of people from the neighbourhood. It had become a regular thing. Strangers would open up, talk about their lives with these three crazy Canadians.

But had Jennifer been hinting of deeper feelings? Feelings she had for him? Was it possible? Again Glen tugged at the collar of his sweatshirt. He couldn't stop sweating. Confusion had taken over. What did he want?

Glen shifted his weight on the dainty chair. He scanned the shoppers, the office workers, the hipsters, coming down the sidewalk. He checked his watch again. Hank had said he'd be back by three o'clock. Again Glen peered into the passing crowd, searching for Hank's familiar face.

Glen felt a tap on his knee. "Mister?" A little girl had stopped in front of him. She looked up into Glen's face. "Where's the elf?"

The child wore a pair of earmuffs on her small head. Her hand was being held by an older child, a boy.

Glen grinned at the little girl. "Aren't I a good enough elf? See my hat?"

The girl stared at him, her face set.

"No? Well…" Glen pointed over to Nick, who was down by the alley feeding pigeons. "Is that him?" The girl's gaze followed Glen's pointing finger. Nick stood surrounded by a sea of grey birds pecking the sidewalk. The girl shook her curls.

"Where's my elf? He said he would be here till Christmas."

"Does your elf have a big brown mustache?"

She nodded her head.

"Is he dressed in green pants and red suspenders?"

Again she nodded, her curls bouncing. "Bubba and I are going to the toy store. It's the biggest toy store in the whole world. Santa is going to be there."

But now the child was being yanked away, pulled along by her 'Bubba.'

Glen waved a little wave, and leaned back. He tipped the chair on its hind legs. He was remembering Jennifer's words: "I'd like to start a family…" Again Glen began to sweat. He felt confused. It was all happening so fast. Sure, he had a crush on Jennifer. What man wouldn't?

At that moment something cracked under him. The chair tilted sideways as he jumped to his feet. "Oh dear." How was he going to explain this to Hank?

Glen righted the walnut chair, but it tilted again. There was a split in one of the slender carved legs. Maybe it could be glued before Hank returned.

"Nick?" Glen called over the heads of people passing on the sidewalk. "Hey, do we have any glue?" But Nick was still playing the flute to his damn pigeons.

Glen got down on his hands and knees by the little chair. It was a bad break. Maybe he could wrap the split leg with some twine. At that moment he caught sight of a woman's ankles. They were trim ankles, above small flat shoes. A woman's voice called down to him in a soft lilt. "You are looking for something? You have lost… what they call a 'contact'?"

Glen was still down on his hands and knees. Now he scrambled heavily to his feet. "A contact lens? You mean for…" and he pointed at his eyes. "No, no, I don't need glasses. No…" He looked mournfully down at Hank's chair. It still tilted on its back leg. "I was just seeing if I could fix this," he muttered.

The woman held out a clothes hanger. "I brought your sweater."

"My sweater!" It was folded neatly over the hanger and covered with clear plastic.

"It is very pretty. It is made by hand knit?"

"Yes." They both stared at the sweater's pattern of snowflakes and reindeer. Glen tried to explain. "Handling the trees, the pitch is sticky." He reached for his wallet. "Let me pay you."

"You already paid, you don't remember?" The woman's warm smile had a touch of shyness to it. She looked around at the trees. "It is very pretty here. It smells so nice." She pressed her nose into one of the wreaths hung by the doorway. She breathed deeply, eyes closed. "All day I breathe the fumes from the dry cleaning."

Glen looked again at his sweater folded on the hanger. He shook his head in wonder. "I can't believe you brought my sweater over. This is very special service."

"I thought you would need it. It is my coffee break."

Then Glen really looked at her. She wore only a plain dress of dark wool gathered at the waist. "But you're not wearing a coat. You'll catch your death!"

"What does that mean, please? I am still learning English."

"Catch your death? It means... well, it means you might get sick, get a cold."

She smiled up at him. "And I will die?" she teased. She was a very short woman, with a full bosom. Her black hair was pulled back from her face. Her skin was light brown. She had wide cheekbones, and black eyes. Right now they sparkled with mischief. "In my country, we do not speak of catching death. Death, he catches us."

Glen stared down at her. This woman had such a calm presence. There was a beauty in her face that shone from deep within. She seemed to know exactly who she was. And exactly who *he* was.

"But how did you know where to find me?"

She merely waited for him to answer his own question.

"Of course!" and he smacked his forehead. "You work right over there." He pointed across 7th Avenue. "The Quik-Stop Dry Cleaners. Probably have a great view of us over here."

The woman only smiled.

Glen leaned forward, his voice earnest. "Have you bought your Christmas tree yet?"

She laughed, shaking her head. "I have no room. Where I live there is no room."

Glen's brow furrowed in concern. "No room for a Christmas tree?" He picked up a Charlie Brown, one of the little three-foot trees.

She laughed. "No, that is too big."

"Too big? A Charlie Brown? How small is your apartment?"

"Small," she nodded.

"Too small to even change your mind in?"

"Change my mind?" She smiled up at him. "You are funny. You are like a clown."

"I am? Oh, you mean this hat?" He pulled it off. "Now do I look like a clown?"

Her smile widened. She nodded, and couldn't help but laugh. It was a warm, lingering laugh.

For some reason, Glen didn't mind being laughed at by her. "What about some branches? Here, take these." He scooped up an armful. The branches had been trimmed from the bottom of a balsam fir.

She looked at them with longing.

"Go on, they're free. Here… Put out your arms."

But instead she fingered the needles on a branch. "I must go back to work now." She pinched the needles between her fingers and brought the scent to her nose. Again she closed her eyes, as if to shut out all but that aroma of forest.

Glen watched her, this short, nicely-plump woman. Then he said, "Do you mind if I ask where you're from?"

"You mean my country? My old country is Peru. I am from the mountains there, the Andes."

Glen still held his armful of branches. "Jeez." He wagged his head in disbelief. "Peru… You could knock me over with a feather."

She knit her brows, trying to understand. She sized up Glen's bulk. She was obviously confused.

"Don't worry. It's just a saying. It means that I'm very impressed."

"You are impressed I am from Peru?"

He studied her face, with its wide cheekbones and warm dark eyes.

She felt his stare. "I am Magda." And she ducked her head, with that touch of shyness again.

"I'm from the mountains, too," Glen gushed, talking fast. "From Canada." He wanted to distract her from her own shyness. "I'm just a country bumpkin like yourself. A bumpkin—that means, it means..."

Guilty thoughts were racing through Glen's head. Coming to New York, he'd dared to have hopes that maybe he'd meet a woman—the right woman. He'd even prayed to Saint Jude. *Please, Saint Jude, match me up with one of the millions of women who pray to you for a husband.* But everything seemed to be happening so fast. This woman, Magda...

And only this morning, Jennifer had confided her feelings to him. She was obviously serious about him. But what she'd said had caught Glen totally by surprise.

Sure, he'd had a crush on Jennifer. He always got crushes on women if they talked to him. It's just that they'd never liked him in the same way. They just wanted to be "friends." How many times had he heard that in his life?

At the moment he was still holding the branches in his arms, his Christmas hat back on his head. A million thoughts raced through his brain. But he couldn't think of a thing to say, except to blurt, "My name is Glen."

The woman called Magda was still looking down at the side-walk. "And your last name is Turner."

Glen's jaw dropped. Who was this woman? A mind reader? Was she reading his thoughts? Glen gulped. "How do you know my last name?"

She smiled up at him. She pointed to the sweater, newly cleaned. "Your name is on the ticket."

Mr. Baxter

Mr. Baxter looked around. It was hard to believe that a woman had ever lived with him in this apartment. He never spoke of his wife to anyone. He never spoke her name aloud. He didn't like to think about it. No trace remained of that brief, shared happiness. Thirty years later, there were none of her clothes left in the closet. The medicine cabinet in the bathroom held only his razor and shaving cream and a single toothbrush.

But about 10 years ago, he'd found a single bobby pin behind the toilet. The bobby pin had been wedged between two floorboards all those years. Mr. Baxter had picked up the bobby pin. It was made of black metal; his wife's hair had been black.

Pain had then twisted inside his chest. For a moment he'd thought he might be having a heart attack. He'd gasped a few breaths, and tried to slow the painful pounding of his heart.

Then he'd taken the bobby pin into the living room and held it under the reading lamp. Where were his glasses?

With trembling fingers Mr. Baxter had put his glasses on. Again he'd picked up the bobby pin, and peered at it under the circle of light. A black strand of hair was caught in the pin.

That's when his wife's name had slipped from his tongue in a whisper.

5

December 18

The dawn broke with a cold, bitter wind. The wind coursed down 7th Avenue. It swirled dust and grit from the streets. Litter from the gutters and the trash baskets was lifted and blown against the Christmas trees at the corner.

The wind whistled as it blew, and the notes from Nick's pan-flute were quickly lifted away, lost. Whenever Nick worked the early morning shift, he greeted the dawn with his flute.

Hank and Glen were still asleep in the van. The sky had already grown lighter. The streetlamps blinked off, all at once.

The last note lifted from Nick's flute and was swirled away in a gust of wind. Slowly he raised his head, blinking. The dust of the street stung his eyes. "Hey, Texas Eddy," he called out. He stood waiting as Eddy trudged toward him, leaning into the wind.

"Eddy, my friend..." Nick held up his hand. Eddy held up his, the fingers grimy with dirt. They gave each other the "high-five," slapping their hands together in the greeting of the street.

Eddy wore a black knit cap. It was pulled down low over his brow, and covered his ears. He smiled at Nick, but it was a grimace of missing teeth. "You-all need anything?"

Nick shook his head. He pulled him into the little shelter. Trees leaned against the outside of the hut. The thick branches muffled the shriek of the wind for those inside. And the heater warmed the little room.

"Sit down, Eddy. Here." Nick lifted a pile of laundry from the only chair. It was a battered kitchen chair. It had chrome metal legs. Its seat and backrest were covered in faded red plastic. Eddy regarded the chair with pride. He'd found it in one of the green dumpsters in the neighbourhood. It was a replacement for the walnut chair that had broken under Glen's weight.

"You want some coffee, Eddy?" Nick lifted the lid of the kettle. The coffee's aroma filled the little hut. The smell itself seemed to cheer both men. They held their cups with both hands, warming them. The plastic tarp above their heads rippled noisily.

"How's business, Eddy? You don't look so good."

"I'm needing a light here." Eddy's pale eyes were tired. His nose was runny and his face was pinched from the cold. A cigarette butt dangled from his cracked lips.

Nick struck a match. He leaned over and lit the cigarette's blackened tip. Then he sat back on the edge of the table. "Where'd you sleep last night, Eddy?"

Eddy pulled a long drag of smoke into his lungs. His face relaxed. "It's nice in here. You folks have a nice place." He ignored Nick's question, or perhaps he hadn't heard it.

"Eddy, tell me something. How long ago did you leave Texas?" Nick waited. "You hear me, Eddy?"

But Eddy was still counting. He took another puff and held it. "Twenty-three years," his voice squeezed out, with a wisp of smoke.

Nick was quiet for a while. Then, "Eddy, where you gonna be on Christmas Day?"

"When's that?"

"It's a week away."

Eddy shrugged, and took another drag on his cigarette. He squinted at Nick through the smoke. "So where will you be?"

"That's what I'm getting to, Eddy. On Christmas Day, I fly back to Canada. And in Canada I got my little house in the woods, no phone, no electricity to pay. I got trees all around, clean air. I got deer coming out of the forest to eat an apple out of my hand." Nick looked down at the tattered rug that covered the subway grate. He sighed. "I hate thinking that you'll still be here, living on the street." He lifted his dark gaze, to meet Eddy's pale eyes. "Maybe it's time you went back to Texas."

Eddy slowly turned his head to the side. His eyes were half-closed.

"Eddy, forget your pride. This ain't no way to live. Why don't you go back? You can't work any harder than you do now, right?"

"You got some sugar for this coffee?"

Nick stirred in one spoonful. Eddy waited. Nick stirred in another. Eddy waited. "You want more?" At his nod, Nick stirred in a third heaping spoonful.

"More."

Nick stirred in spoonful number four. "That's it, Eddy. This stuff will kill you." Nick closed the bag of sugar and set it back on the table.

The cold wind was finding its way into the hut. Nick poured himself some more coffee.

"Eddy, let me ask you something."

"Is this more advice?" Eddy's eyelids fluttered. He appeared to doze for a moment.

"No, man. You do what you're gonna do." Nick set his empty cup down. "No, it's something that's been bothering me these last days. Let me ask you something. You've heard of this disease, AIDS, am I right?

"Of course." Eddy straightened in the chair. His pale eyes blinked. His mind seemed to focus. "But AIDS isn't really a disease."

"No?"

"I read about it over at Saint Vinny's. I was waiting in the Emergency Room." Eddy leaned forward. "Some guy cut me on the subway. Right by my thumb." He spit on his hand and rubbed away the dirt, revealing a long red scar with the stitches still in. "The blood wouldn't stop pumping. I had to hold the damn thing shut for two hours."

"Yeah, it looks bad. So, Eddy, tell me what you read over there."

Eddy tapped his brow with a dirty finger. "I have a photographic memory. That's why I can find you anything in this city. You just ask, I know where I saw it last." He glanced around the hut. "You need anything?"

"Eddy, you're gonna come to the point soon, right? I gotta go clean up outside for the customers. A load of trees came in last night."

Eddy didn't seem to hear him. He was staring above Nick's head at a point in space. His pale eyes were half closed. He was reading from memory the poster he'd seen on the hospital wall. "...AIDS is a condition that lowers the body's resistance to infection. It allows a variety of diseases to attack the body..." Eddy's eyelids drooped.

"That's great, Eddy." Nick reached out and patted his knee. "But what I want to know is, what's your take on this AIDS thing? People here, they're walking the streets covered with sores. You think this is some kind of punishment on the human race? You think we got off track somewhere?"

Eddy jerked awake from a doze.

Nick started to pace the tiny room. He waved the smoke aside. "I got a lotta things on my mind, Eddy. I got another question for you. There's a beggar I seen around here a lotta times. That big black guy, shaking his tomato can, using a crutch. You know him? You know who I'm talking about?"

Eddy nodded.

"Then let me ask you something, Eddy. Let me ask you this."

Nick looked down at the rug for a moment, then looked up. "Is he for real?"

"What do you mean?"

Nick shrugged one shoulder. "What I'm asking—is the guy really a cripple?"

Eddy's pale, sleepy eyes came into focus. "You mean does he need the crutch?" He tried to think. "No, I guess not."

"Does this guy live on the street? Is he homeless?"

"No. He drives back to Long Island every night."

"So shaking the tomato can..."

Eddy's eyelids fluttered. "That's how he makes his living. He's got a family to feed."

Nick slowly nodded. "All right. Okay. That's good enough for me."

But Eddy had fallen asleep. His head lolled to one side. His cigarette had become a long ash curving down.

"Eddy, wake up. Come on, stand up. Here's eight, nine... here's 10 bucks from the kitty." Nick pressed the bills into Eddy's fingers. "Go rent yourself a room, get some sleep."

Eddy swayed on his feet. "Tell me about Canada again, about the woods."

"You get some rest first. I got work to do."

By one o'clock that afternoon, the wind had died down. Hank was taking a nap in the van. At least he was trying to. In reality, he lay awake, tormented by his conscience.

I should have gone right to the police. I was witness to a murder... But what did I actually see? I saw no face that I could identify...

His daughter's face then came to mind as he lay there. Celia's face was such an innocent face, so beautiful. She'd cried when she'd learned that Hank was leaving for a month. "What about Christmas, Daddy?"

Hank turned on his side. *After all, I would never be able to pick out the killers in a police lineup. All I heard was that strange sound, and the muffled shot—and then that black limo pulled away.*

Hank finally gave up trying to sleep. He climbed from the van, out into the hut.

After a quick splash of water to his face, he emerged to the sidewalk, blinking. The sidewalk was littered with trash from the windstorm. Hank reached for the broom. As he did so, a long black limousine pulled into the alley.

Hank froze. His hands tightened around the broom handle. It was a long black limousine with dark-tinted windows, exactly like the one that night.

The driver stepped out into the alley, and opened the back door for his passenger.

A dark, heavy-set man emerged. A cashmere overcoat was draped over his shoulders. He adjusted the sleeves of his suit. It was a well-cut suit. His cufflinks flashed gold in the pale sunlight. The wind had finally spent itself. There was not the slightest breeze to ruffle the man's silk tie. Not a single hair on the man's dark head was out of place. He was obviously a man used to getting his own way.

The man was approaching. He walked with his chin held high. He didn't seem to notice the orange extension cord across the sidewalk. There was no chance for Hank to call a warning. He couldn't even open his mouth. The cord was usually taped down to the sidewalk, but it had worked loose under so much foot traffic.

The toe of the man's shiny black shoe slipped under the cord.

Hank held his breath. But the man in the expensive suit only tripped slightly and caught himself—and kept coming. He looked straight at Hank. "Who do I sue here?" he asked, in a thick New York accent.

Glen hurried over. He was frowning. "What happened? Who pulled the plug? We've lost all our power."

It was true. The Christmas lights on the big display tree no longer blinked their colours. And the overhead light bulbs were off.

Hank thrust the broom at Glen. "I'll go."

Hank followed the path of the orange electric cord. At the alley, it turned left, and passed a row of overflowing garbage cans. Then it ran up a step and through a small round hole at the bottom of a door.

Hank followed it, opening the door. He was greeted with clouds of steam and cooking smells and the noise of many voices speaking in Chinese. The cord's plug lay on the floor by the outlet. Hank plugged it in again, and slipped out.

Outside, he leaned against the door of the Chinese restaurant. His heart was still racing in fear. He looked up at the pale sky. Electric wires crossed overhead in all directions. Where could he run from the murderers? Nowhere.

He walked slowly back down the alley.

The man in the expensive suit was talking to Glen, who listened intently. His head bobbed up and down in agreement. And when Glen spied Hank, he hailed him. "Hank, this gentleman is having a Christmas party. He'd like to rent six trees, along with their stands. It's just for the day. You think that's okay? Where's Nick?"

"I don't know," Hank muttered as he edged past the man in the suit.

"Hold on there." The man put his hand on Hank's arm. "Don't take me serious. I don't plan to sue."

Hank dared a glance into the man's dark eyes. Were they the eyes of a killer? They were dark and shining. The man nudged Hank in the ribs. "Hey, let's see a little of the Christmas spirit."

There was alcohol on the man's breath, but he wasn't drunk. He was very much in control. He turned back to Glen and pointed. "Give me a dozen of those wreaths." He drew a shiny leather wallet from an inside pocket of his overcoat. "So... 12 wreaths and six Douglas firs with their stands..." He peeled off three $100 bills. Then he eyed Glen, who wore a worried frown.

The man peeled off two more 100's. "Is that enough?"

Glen's frown disappeared. "Don't worry, sir. You'll get most of this back when you return the trees."

The man leveled a glance at Glen, then Hank. With a faint smile he said, "I'm not worried." There was a hint of threat in his voice.

Glen tied the trees to the roof of the limousine. "Hank, can you give me a hand here?" They stuffed the wreaths and stands into the trunk.

Glen watched the limo drive off. He stood with his hands on his hips. "Jeez. Do you think he belongs to the Mafia?"

Hank didn't answer. He picked up the broom again.

"Hank? Is anything wrong? Are you still mad at me about your chair?"

Hank was pushing the broom down the sidewalk toward the alley. He stopped. He seemed dazed. "Chair?"

"The chair! The fancy chair you found! The chair I sat on and broke!"

"Oh."

"Hank, what's going on with you? You've been acting so strange lately. You're not yourself." Glen's round face wore an earnest expression. The flaps of his Christmas hat hung down over his ears. "What is it? Tell me what's going on."

Hank turned the broom in the opposite direction, towards Greenwich Avenue. The broom pushed litter ahead of it along the sidewalk. Glen followed at Hank's side. "I've been your friend for 20-odd years, Hank. If you can't talk to me, then who can you talk—" Glen stopped. Hank stopped.

A man was running towards them from across Greenwich. The man's knees pumped high. He was running fast. He darted back and forth among the people using the crosswalk. "Stop him!" screamed a woman's hoarse voice. "He stole my purse!"

Heads turned. People were taken by surprise as the thief ran past.

When he reached the Christmas tree lot, he hesitated. Trees lined the sidewalk on either side. The path between was now blocked by Glen and Hank. Their faces looked as surprised as the thief's.

Without thinking, Hank lunged for the man's waist. They fell together to the sidewalk. The thief tried to crawl away as Hank clung to him. He squirmed over onto his back and began kicking. The strap of the stolen purse was twisted around his arm.

That's when Glen sat on him. He sat down heavily on his chest and pinned his arms to the sidewalk. "That wasn't very nice of you, stealing a woman's purse."

By now a crowd had gathered. "Bravo!" People began to clap and cheer. A woman in the crowd opened her briefcase and pulled out a cell-phone. "I'm calling the cops," she announced to more cheers. It was a happy crowd, brought together by the victory of simple good over simple evil.

Glen smiled up at the onlookers. "Only seven more shopping days till Christmas, folks."

Laughter rippled through the crowd.

"Get off me you big—" The thief spit curses at Glen. Hank still clung to the legs of the man, who was trying to kick him off. Hank now turned his face to one side. His Canada hat fell to the sidewalk, exposing the bald spot at the back of his head.

Glen continued to chat with the crowd of people. Many were Christmas shoppers and carried armloads of packages. "Has everyone bought their Christmas tree? If not, we've got some beauties right over there."

The mugger turned and twisted under him.

"Whoa!" cried Glen, riding him.

Then a woman stepped from the crowd. She leaned down and quietly tugged at the strap of the purse. She pulled it free. With the toe of her pointed shoe she jabbed the thief in the ribs. Then without a word she walked off, with the purse under her arm.

"You're welcome," Glen called after her. She didn't look back. She merely hurried her step, crossing 7th Avenue.

"Did you get him? Where's my purse?" An elderly woman now hobbled across Greenwich. She had waited for the next green light. "Did you get my purse?"

Glen looked up at her, confused. The thief still twisted under him, even with Hank holding the man's legs.

The old woman cried out in a hoarse voice. "I don't care about this low-down scum! Where's my purse?"

A policeman walking his beat parted the crowd. "What's going on here?"

When Nick finally returned he was greeted with excitement. "Nick!" cried Glen. "You'll never guess what happened!"

But Nick paid little attention. He was beaming. "Listen to this. I got a new word: Be-nev-o-lent."

"Nick! We caught a thief!"

Nick's face fell. "What was he after?" In a low voice he added, "Did he find the kitty?"

Glen followed Nick into the hut. "No, no. The guy was a purse-snatcher."

Nick reached up behind the food shelf. He brought down a fat sock and opened it, looking in. "So he didn't get the boss's money. Good, good... Yeah, sorry about being late. I took one of the three-footers over to Saint Vinny's. I figured they could use a bit of Christmas in the Emergency Ward." Nick smiled up at Glen. "You should have seen their faces when I brought in that tree. Man, their eyes lit up, you know what I mean?"

"Nick—"

"And I took a couple of Scotch pines down to the church. I told the priest they're for persons who can't afford to buy a tree. We got to talking, me and the priest. He said I was doing a be-nev-o-lent act. That's the word. I gotta look it up in my dictionary. Where'd I put it?" He found the little book. "Yeah, I'm gonna surprise Kate, right? Be-nev-o-lent. Here it is."

Hank stood in the doorway. "Tell him the rest," he said in a flat voice.

"The rest?" Glen thought for a moment. "Oh—and a guy came by in a big limo."

Nick listened with interest as Glen filled him in. Then Glen added, "So, does he sound like he's in the Mafia?"

A loud horn blasted right outside. It honked in a familiar rhythm. No one moved.

"That must be the boss."

The horn honked again, impatient.

Nick pulled out the sock again. He took out the roll of bills. His eyes widened at the five 100's.

"That's from the Mafia guy," Glen explained. "That's his deposit. We'd better keep those."

"How much are we charging him to rent six trees?"

"I... I didn't mention any exact figure."

More honking from outside.

"What about stands? You rented him stands?"

Glen nodded. "And he took some wreaths."

"Did he buy the wreaths or just rent them? We don't want Mr. Hammer coming down on us, saying we got short-changed."

Hank was elected to go face Mr. Hammer. Out at the curb, he knocked gently at the back window of the station wagon. No response. Mr. Hammer sat slumped with his head back. His mouth hung open. He was snoring. It looked like he hadn't shaved in a week.

Hank then knocked at the driver's window. Mr. Hammer's pimply-faced son rolled down the window. Hank was about to give the rolls of bills to the boy when a hand reached from the back seat. "I'll take that."

Then the back door of the station wagon opened. Hank knew that the open door wasn't an invitation to join the boss in the back seat. It was a command. He climbed in.

"Shut the door. You raised in a barn?" Hammer counted the bills. Then he counted them all a second time. "Is this it? Is this all you got to show for the last 24 hours?"

Hank nodded. He felt trapped.

"You guys gotta do better. You're too soft, too nice. Don't let the customer bargain for his tree. *You* set the price. And don't let some slut bat her eyes at you to a get a tree on the cheap. You hear?"

Hank sighed. "Yes, sir."

Hammer called forward to the boy at the wheel. "You hear that, kid? This guy has manners. You could learn something."

Hammer's wild laugh filled the car. He leaned back on the seat, and turned his haggard face towards Hank. "You have any trouble yet with people stealing trees?"

Hank smiled to himself, remembering the "bear" he'd chased away that first night. "No," he answered.

"Well, this is what you do. You get a pipe or a baseball bat. Beat the crap out of them. Break an arm, break a leg. Mess them up a little."

"Yes, Mr. Hammer." Hank put his hand on the door handle.

"Go, go. I gotta get some sleep." Hammer pulled up the collar of his black-and-white checked jacket. He sank down in the seat, eyes closed.

"Wait!"

Hank sat back again.

Eyes still closed, the boss gave him a last warning. "A tree lot down in Soho was torched last night. Burned to the ground, every tree. Of course, the fellow running it didn't work for me. He thought he could do it on his own." Hammer opened one eye. "Without my protection, you understand?" And the eye closed.

Hank stepped from the station wagon. He wanted to slam the door shut as hard as he could. New York was getting to him. Nothing was simple here. Today he'd saved an old woman's purse from being stolen. And then another woman had stolen the same purse right off the thief! She'd done it in plain sight of everyone. And just walked off—disappeared into the Christmas crowds with the purse under her arm. What kind of a person would do that?

Hank was standing there on the curb, shaking his head, when someone tapped him on the shoulder. "Young man?"

Hank turned to face a woman of about 60 years with bleached-blonde hair. Her worn face was lined with worry. She pointed over to the hut, to the Christmas tree lot. "I believe you're one of the fellows who works here?"

"Yes, ma'am."

She opened the coin purse in her hands. "I'm going to visit my son over at the hospital. I was hoping you might watch the meter for me. And if it runs out, you could feed it these quarters." She looked into Hank's eyes. "I can tell you're a good person."

Hank shifted on his feet. "Well, I used to think so…" He accepted the handful of coins.

"That should be enough. Right now the meter's good for an hour. But I'll be gone longer than that." The woman looked away for a moment. Tears sprang to her eyes. "You see, my son has AIDS." She nodded, "Um-hmm," pressing her lips together. "AIDS," she repeated. She turned to look at Hank. "Yes, you see, Saint Vincent's Hospital is the main AIDS hospital in New York City. Yes, my son, he's only… well, he's about your age. Still young," she murmured.

Then she squared her shoulders. "That's my car over there, the blue sedan."

"All right." Hank slipped the quarters into the pocket of his green wool knickers. "Don't worry," he called after her. "I'll take care of it for you."

The quarters jingled in Hank's pocket. They wouldn't let him forget. He kept recalling the woman's pitiful face. But business was steady that afternoon. Customers kept stopping by, looking for the perfect tree. He had no time to dwell on the mother's plight. But the quarters jingled in his pants pocket, like a sad little tune.

During a lull in business, Glen approached Hank with his Christmas hat in one hand. "Hank? You mind if I make a quick dash over to the dry cleaners? I got a spot of pitch on one of my earflaps. It's okay? You'll be okay here?"

"Go, go," Hank waved him on.

"I'll be right back," Glen called over his shoulder. He hurried to catch the green light across 7th.

For the last week, Glen had been feeling terribly guilty. It had to do with Jennifer. She'd been stopping by the hut every day, on her way to and from rehearsal. And every day she seemed happier than the day before. Even Nick had remarked on it. "She seems to be in love," is what he'd said. And Glen could only gulp, "I know." How could he tell Jennifer that he didn't share her feelings?

He was in a bind. If he crossed the street to visit Magda, he'd be cheating on Jennifer. It was that simple. But now he had to get his hat cleaned.

Reaching the other side of 7th, Glen paused by the lamppost. He was wearing clean grey sweat pants and his reindeer sweater. He ran a hand over his hair. Again he began to question himself. He'd always thought of himself as a romantic fellow, pining after this woman and that woman. But was he capable of really loving someone? Was he? Maybe he didn't have a heart after all.

Well, he'd have to find out. And then he'd have to explain things to Jennifer somehow.

Glen pushed open the door to Quik-Stop Dry Cleaners. The bell jangled overhead. He held the door open for a customer going out. The bell jangled again as the door closed. Glen was alone in the shop. He laid his Christmas hat on the counter. On the counter was a small silver dome: a little bell to press for service. He stared down at it. He felt guilt and excitement, mixed. Should he press the bell?

"Hello," came a calm voice, with a soft accent.

Glen smiled. "Hello, Magda." Just hearing her voice, a peace came over him.

"What is this?" With deft fingers she picked up the fleece hat. She smiled up at him. "This is your clown hat?" Her dark eyes danced with mischief.

Glen flushed. He pointed to the ear flap. "There's a spot of pitch on it."

Magda inspected the hat. "There is no…"

"The pitch must be on the other flap, I'm sure it's there." Glen's words stumbled over each other.

Magda looked up at him. "I see." Her smile had grown shy. It was her turn to become flustered.

He pointed to green hat now lying limp on the counter. "When will it be ready?"

Magda fingered the fleece hat. She'd ducked her head. *Was she laughing at him again?*

She wore a white blouse with a wide scooped neckline. Her warm brown skin looked so smooth. A small gold cross hung at her throat. Glen could see the pulse of her heart, right where the necklace lay against her skin.

"Jeez, it's warm in here," Glen exclaimed, looking around. He could hear the big steam pressing machines at work in the back of the shop. The front windows were all steamed up.

Magda clutched the green fleece hat to her chest. It seemed as if she'd decided something. "Mr. Turner?" Their eyes met.

"Glen, call me Glen."

"I will bring it to you. On my way home."

"That's perfect!" he grinned, and reached for his wallet.

Magda held up her hand. "No, there is no cost."

Glen didn't walk back across the street, he floated. Surely his feet didn't touch the pavement.

Things were busy over at the Christmas tree lot. Hank caught sight of Glen, and called to him. "Could you run this tree through the wrapper? I've got another customer waiting."

The boom box was playing. As Glen worked, he hummed along to "Deck the Halls" and "We Three Kings." The lights of the display tree blinked their colours and brightened the late-afternoon gloom. Glen lifted the wrapped tree to the waiting customer. "Merry Christmas!"

"I'm Jewish," came the reply.

"Oh! Well then, Happy Hanukkah to you, sir!"

Glen's ears were turning red from the cold. They were missing the hat with the earflaps. But his spirits were high. He kept checking his watch. When did Magda get off work?

Between customers, Hank was keeping an eye on the parking meter. At 2:30 he walked over to the blue sedan and fed an hour's worth of quarters into the meter. At 3:30 he did the same. He scanned the sidewalks for the woman with the bleached-blonde hair. There was no sign of her. Hank couldn't forget her worried face, and the sadness in her eyes. He walked back. There were still two quarters left, clinking together in his pocket.

At five o'clock, Hank started feeding his own quarters into the meter. He stood for a moment by the blue sedan and searched the crowded sidewalks. It was getting dark. On a building up on 7th, a display of Christmas lights blinked on. It was a tall building. The white lights glittered in a huge design. Hank tugged at his mustache, frowning. Where was she? Why was she taking so long?

At six o'clock, a tall black man showed up at the Christmas tree lot. He was drunk, happily drunk, as he bought a 10-foot balsam fir. Everything was a joke, everything was funny. "You ever seen a sweater like this here sweater?" he asked Glen. Large yellow and black stripes crossed his chest. "Don't I look jus' like a bee—a big ol' bumble bee? Don't I?"

Glen pulled the big fir through the tree wrapper. He knew what was coming. This guy was in no shape to carry his tree home. He was going to need it delivered. Glen checked his watch. Where was Magda? Didn't she get off work soon?

The man plucked at Glen's shoulder. "That's a hot sweater you got there yourself. Those are deer, right? What say you and me make a trade?"

"No way," said Glen. "My sister knit this."

"Your sister?" The man threw back his head as a belly laugh rocked him.

It was a wonderful laugh, and Glen couldn't help but smile. But he cast a look around. "Hank? Nick? Can somebody else take care of this delivery?"

"No, no," laughed the fellow in the bumble bee sweater. He pointed a long finger at Glen. "*You* bring it." And he wandered off down the sidewalk, turning the corner down Greenwich.

There was nothing else to do. Glen hefted the tree to his shoulder. At the curb, he cast a last glance across 7th. That's when he saw Magda.

She was crossing with the green light while the traffic waited. She took her time coming across. People hurried past her, but Magda walked at her own pace. She walked as if she were crossing a field, not a busy six-lane street. She was short, and her coat was too big for her, too long. But it didn't seem to matter. She knew who she was.

"Magda!" Glen shouted. It felt so good to call out her name. He stood waiting, balancing the tree on his right shoulder. With his teeth he pulled off his left glove and stuffed it into his pocket. Then he held out his hand. "Come with me." His thick fingers closed around Magda's small plump hand.

She didn't ask where they were going. She simply quickened her step to keep up. Their breath clouded in the cold evening air as they walked.

"See that man walking up ahead in the striped sweater?"

"I see him."

"Well, this is his tree."

"I am kidnapped?" There was a sparkle in Magda's eyes.

Glen didn't dare look down at her. He thought his chest would burst from happiness. For the first block they walked along in silence. At the curb, Glen murmured, "Your hand is so warm."

Magda laughed. "It is your hand that is hot."

Back at the Christmas tree lot, Hank kept watch over the parking meter as promised. It was past six and dark when the blonde woman finally returned. He saw her standing at the door to her car. Her visit to the hospital had lasted almost five hours.

Hank walked over. "Ma'am, are you all right?"

The woman turned. The car keys were in her hand. She didn't seem to know who he was. Her haggard face was tear-stained. Her eyes were reddened and wide with grief.

"I'm the fellow you gave the quarters to," Hank explained. He spoke as gently as he could. He didn't want her to be afraid that he was a mugger or anything. But she wasn't afraid. She seemed to be looking right through him with her haggard, tired eyes.

"Are you sure you're all right to drive? You look pretty shaky."

When she didn't answer, he added, "How is your son?"

The woman dropped her keys. She held out her arms in the most pitiful way.

She didn't cry as Hank held her. She only shook, her whole body shaking. Hank swallowed the lump in his throat. He held the perfect stranger until her shaking stopped.

Then he picked up her keys from the sidewalk. He unlocked the door for her, and held her elbow as she stepped into the blue sedan.

It had already been a 10-minute walk for Glen and Magda. They'd reached Washington Square. The man in the bumble bee sweater had stopped to talk with a doorman in front of a fancy building. He and the doorman appeared to be old friends. The black man's wonderful drunken laughter rang out. He shook the doorman's hand, and passed into the lobby of the building. Glen and Magda followed with the tree.

The lobby gleamed with marble and polished brass.

The 10-foot Christmas tree wouldn't fit into the elevator at first. They had to bend the crown. The balsam's wonderful smell filled the elevator as they all rode up. Six, seven, eight... The fellow stepped out at the top floor. He wasn't so drunk now. He was able to fit his key into the lock. He chuckled to himself. "My father, hoo-ee, he's gonna be so surprised, he sees this tree."

Then he pushed open the huge oak door to reveal an elegant hallway.

Glen lowered the tree from his shoulder.

"No, no! Come on in and have a beer. My father must have a beer or two in his fridge."

Glen hesitated. "You don't live here?"

"Me!" the man cried. "My father would kick my butt if he knew I was here. He don't know I still got a key." The black man pulled off his big yellow and black striped sweater and threw it onto a chair. "Bring that tree on in to the living room."

"Well..." Glen glanced down at Magda. She stood quietly with her arms folded across her chest. "Should we take our shoes off?"

"Your shoes off?" That laugh rang out again, within the large beautiful room. "You must have us mixed up with the Japanese. The *Japanese* take their shoes off. No, no, my father is *black*, you understand? He is black and *rich*. Here, come over here, lady. Take a look at this view."

Magda walked over in her long coat. She joined the man at the window, looking out. The sparkle of lights danced beyond. "Where is your father?" she asked quietly.

Glen came to stand beside Magda. He didn't look at the view itself. He looked at his and Magda's reflection. Her small, still form beside his large bulk. They were like two shadow-ghosts. The lights of the city sparkled through them.

"What does it matter where my father is?" The man waved his arm. "He's off somewhere in Europe, doing his thing. My father's a very important man."

Glen took Magda by the elbow. "We should go."

"Oh no you don't! You ain't leaving without this." He reached in his pocket and held up two $10 bills. He smacked them down into Glen's hand and covered it with his own. "Eku odun. You know what that means?"

"No sir, I don't."

"Well now you do." He laughed a sad laugh. "It means 'Merry Christmas' in the Yoruban language."

Riding down in the elevator, Magda was quiet. Finally she murmured something to herself. Glen leaned his head down. "What?"

"A boy should not be without his father," she repeated. She looked up at him. Sadness shone dark in her eyes.

Glen frowned in concern. "Are you worried about that guy? Why, he had to be 30 years old, at least. He's no boy."

They were almost to the lobby.

"You are wrong, Glen Turner. Tonight he is a boy."

But she let him take her hand as they walked out onto the darkened street.

"Which way?" he asked.

"You will walk me home?"

"Of course." He spoke in earnest. "A woman shouldn't be out alone at night without an escort."

Magda laughed. "You are a funny man. Come, this way."

"You know what I like about you? One of the things? You're never in a hurry. Everybody else in New York is always in a hurry."

To that, Magda giggled.

"Oh jeez, am I walking too fast?"

"My legs are not so high."

Glen slowed his step. "Magda? What if I asked you a personal question?"

"Please, you ask what you like."

"You said you were from Peru."

"Yes," she nodded. "Last I lived in Lima. My husband was not alive when I came here with my boy. Now our son is a grown man. He lives across the bridge, it is a place called Brooklyn." As they passed under a streetlamp she looked up at him. "I live only with myself now. Is that the answer to your question?"

"Wait a minute." Glen let go of her hand. "Sometimes I get sweaty." He wiped his hand on his pants. Then he took Magda's hand again, even though she was laughing at him.

"Now I have *my* question," she said.

"You want to know the difference between Canadians and Americans."

Laughing, she shook her head. "No, no."

"Canadians are funnier than Americans." Glen stopped. He looked at her with his deep-set eyes. "Seriously. Most of the famous comics in the States are from Canada. It's a fact. It's a little-known fact in the States. But it's a well-known fact in Canada."

"This is my building."

"Wait… What about your question? You were going to ask me something."

"I will ask my question another time." From her coat pocket she drew out a small green bundle.

"My hat! I forgot all about it." Glen flushed. "So you found the spot of pitch?" He knew and Magda knew that there had never been any pitch on the hat.

"Bend down," she told him. She pulled the hat onto his head and smiled up at him. "Now you are the funny Canadian."

It had been a busy day at the Christmas tree lot. It was now past seven o'clock, and Nick was hungry. He rolled up the sleeves of his fringed jacket.

Just then Glen arrived, out of breath. He'd trotted all the way back from Magda's building, and his face glowed pink.

"Glennie, where you been? You have trouble on the delivery for that drunk guy?"

Glen stood huffing and puffing, his hands on his hips. He shook his head, No. He leaned over, his hands braced on his knees. "Ran..." he gasped, grinning.

"That's a good way to get yourself a heart attack, Glennie."

Nick wore a headband across his brow. His grey hair was pulled back in a ponytail. Grey wisps had escaped, they hung down over his ears. "I was just gonna go in and start the pasta." He reached into the hut and turned off the boom box. "I can't take any more of those Christmas songs." Then he cocked his head. "Now what?"

Jangle jangle jangle.

The jangling noise grew louder.

"It's your beggar, Nicki."

It was indeed the man with the tomato can, shaking his few coins. The noise ragged on Nick's nerves. *Jangle jangle*. The black man's skin was grey and rough like the hide of an elephant. He struggled along on one crutch. And he stopped right in front of Nick. He shook his can. *Jangle jangle jangle.*

Nick looked up into the man's face, and his eyes narrowed. They stared at each other for a full minute. Neither backed down, or blinked. Finally Nick sighed, and reached for his wallet. He stuffed two dollars into the tomato can. The beggar nodded his thanks, and moved on. His face had remained a blank for the entire stare-down.

By this time, Glen had recovered. He straightened up. "Nick, I don't think I can wait for pasta. How about if I go get us some Chinese food?" Then he called to Hank, up the sidewalk. "How does Chinese sound to you?"

Hank's face was pale under the light bulbs strung overhead.

"What is it, Hank? You look like you've seen a ghost."

"That guy's back."

"What guy?"

"The Mafia guy in the limo. He's got some people with him."

Sure enough, a limousine had pulled into the alley. Several men emerged. One carried a large platter. Another man carried two cardboard boxes stacked in his arms. They were bringing the left-overs from the Christmas party.

When the limo departed, the six rented trees had been returned. They stood on their stands in a row along the sidewalk.

And on the table inside the little hut, a feast was spread on trays and platters. There were tiny pastries stuffed with salmon and crab. And baby carrots cooked in brown sugar. There were shrimp and prawns on toothpicks. There were turkey legs and ham rolls. There was even half a Beef Wellington: a roast covered with mushroom paste inside a baked crust. And of course there were Christmas cookies and tiny mince tarts.

Hank now stood looking down at this spread of food. He was speechless. His eyes were clouded with confusion. He had to step outside, and get some fresh air, and think.

Outside, Hank began pacing the length of the Christmas tree lot. When he reached the alley, he turned and paced back. Was all this food a bribe from the Mafia? Was it supposed to keep him quiet about the murder?

The night life in Greenwich Village had already begun for the evening. The sidewalks were crowded. The clubs and cafes were filling up. When Hank reached the corner at Greenwich Avenue, he suddenly stopped in his tracks. A thought had struck him. Someone bumped into him from behind. "Sorry—" Hank stepped to one side and stood by the lamppost. Then he started to chuckle.

What a fool he'd been. What a stupid fool! Out on the avenue, taxicabs and cars and limousines raced by. Limousines. For it seems there was more than one black limousine in New York City. In fact, at that very moment, another one whizzed past directly in front of him. A black limousine with dark-tinted windows. They couldn't all belong to the Mafia!

Hank turned on his heel. He was hungry and he was going to eat.

Inside the hut, Glen sat on the only chair. He was biting into one of the salmon pastries. Nick held a turkey leg in his fist. He lifted it in greeting to Hank. "What a trip, man. What a trip."

Hank looked at Nick's huge turkey drumstick. He looked at the table covered with fancy food, here in this makeshift hut. And he burst out laughing. It was all so crazy. New York was crazy.

Glen pointed, his mouth full. "Hank, try one of those little crab things." Then Glen raised his eyes to the doorway. "Jennifer!" he blurted with his mouth full. He stood up, cracking his head against the shelf.

"All right, you guys, what's different about me?" Jennifer's face was radiant. "Come on, guess."

Her big bag hung from her shoulder, as usual. And as usual, she was dressed all in black. Black leather jacket, black tights, black high-heeled boots. Jennifer then spied the feast on the table. "Hey, what's all this food? Ooh, it looks delicious... No, no I don't dare. But where'd it come from?"

Hank smiled, chewing. "We have connections."

Jennifer took a single baby carrot and nibbled on it. "Come on, you guys. Look me over. I can't believe you don't see it.

"Nothing has changed," murmured Nick in his husky voice. "You look beautiful."

Hank could only smile, and shrug.

Glen pointed to his mouth: full. But he wasn't chewing. At the sight of Jennifer, a wave of guilt had washed over him. He couldn't put it off any longer. He had to tell Jennifer about Magda. And he had to do it tonight. He had to do it right now.

"Come on, fellas," she pleaded. She held out her left hand, with its long slim fingers. A small diamond ring sparkled. "Take a look. Isn't it beautiful?" She gave an excited little jump. "Dummies! I'm getting married! And you three are the first to know."

Glen's eyes widened, his mouth still full.

"He's my dancing partner," cried Jennifer. "Remember? Remember I told you about the guy who dropped me?"

Mr. Baxter

Mr. Baxter's wife had tried to reason with him. "Lew," she'd said, "terrible things happen in this world. But wonderful things happen too. Darling, you saved that child's life. He's alive because you were there, and you caught him."

But Lew Baxter would remain silent, as he lay beside his wife. He would stare up at the ceiling. And finally he would turn on his side, away from her. He didn't like to be touched anymore. Not since that night.

That night he'd been walking his beat. It had been about eight o'clock, only a few days before Christmas. The year had been 1962. This was going to be Lew Baxter's first Christmas as a married man. He was 40 years old, and he was happy. It was an icy-cold night, with ice crusting the sidewalk. But he was still a young man; he walked with a firm stride, whistling "Silent Night." His breath clouded as it hit the cold air. Silent night, holy night...

There had only been a single scream from the mother, high above Lew Baxter's head. That was his only warning. He'd looked up, three stories, to the fire escape. By some lucky chance, he was in the right place at the right time. It was by instinct that he held out his arms and caught the falling child—caught him, both of them stunned.

And then the second child had come hurtling down.

6

December 22

The phone booth had a door, so Hank closed it against the cold. He rang the number of the office. The Boss wouldn't be there at this time of night, it was almost 11 o'clock. But Mr. Hammer always insisted that they phone in the amount of the day's take. He liked to know exactly how much money he would be picking up the following day. It would be a lot this time. The entire population of New York City was in a frenzy of last-minute Christmas shopping. And that included buying Christmas trees.

The line was ringing at the other end.

In two more days, Hank's stay in New York would be over. Christmas Day he'd be flying home to his daughter. In two more days.

Hank had shut the door of the booth, but he couldn't shut out the cold. He was grateful when the secretary answered.

Leaving the phone booth, Hank saw a few familiar faces in the people walking past. They exchanged nods. Everyone walked with shoulders hunched and hands thrust into their pockets. It was a bitterly cold night. The cold was a special kind of cold. There was a sharpness in the air, almost as if it was going to snow.

Hank hurried up Greenwich Avenue. Reaching 7th, he turned the corner, almost home. He was greeted by the sight of their tall display tree lit up with coloured lights.

As soon as Hank entered the hut, Nick stood to his feet. "I'm beat, Hank. Wake me at three." And he climbed into the van to get some sleep, where Glen was already snoring.

The little hut offered Hank shelter from the cold's sharp bite. It was homey now, crowded with stuff. It seemed like every day Texas Eddy would bring them stuff to buy. There was now a toaster that burned toast. And a pair of old wooden skis leaning in one corner. Hank had bought them from Eddy for 10 bucks.

Hank lit two small candles, even though the lamp was on. Candles added their own kind of warmth. Then he sat on the only chair and began to whittle.

It was close to midnight when the first flakes of snow drifted down. They fell lazily, in large flakes.

Taxicabs still hurtled down 7th Avenue. Sirens screamed. The city at midnight still continued to party, and to murder, at its hurried pace.

The snowflakes seemed to be falling out of an earlier time, when things weren't so hurried. They drifted slowly down, one here, one there, in the freezing air. Slowly they fell, and they didn't melt. In fact, they began to pile up, one on top of the other.

In the hours after midnight, Hank sat and watched. He sat just inside the doorway of the hut, looking out. Silence was slowly falling on New York. Snowflake by snowflake, Hank could hear silence accumulate. The whine of sirens dulled. The rush of traffic down 7th Avenue slowed to a crawl.

Hank lifted the concertina from his lap. He had finally taken it out of his knapsack. Now he unbuckled the leather strap that held the bellows squeezed shut. He fit his gloved hands through the straps on either side of the concertina.

Hank wore his hiking boots and long socks with his green wool knickers. His red suspenders were stretched over three layers of sweaters. His Canada cap was pulled low over his ears.

He played softly. He squeezed the bellows of the concertina in and out. His fingers pressed the small buttons, choosing each note. The melody crooned like a lullaby in the snowy night. Hank was playing only for himself. He played "Greensleeves," to try and soothe his worried thoughts.

Overhead, the string of bare light bulbs shone down. They lit up the little forest of firs and pines. The snow was slowly turning the green branches white. The drone of an airplane passed high above.

Someone walked by as Hank played with his head bent to the music. There was a faint crunch of snow beneath shoes. The footprints left behind were soon filled. The snowflakes fell more thickly now. Hank's tune faded off, finished.

Peals of merry laughter drew his attention. Hank squinted through the falling snow. There was a couple over on Greenwich.

They were throwing snowballs at each other. Hank smiled sadly. He longed to be that carefree again. The falling snow muffled their laughter, yet also seemed to carry it farther.

Then Hank saw something that terrified him almost more than anything else he'd seen in New York. Around the corner came a little girl. Her nightgown hung down below her coat. She shuffled through the snow in bedroom slippers. It was after midnight. And she was alone.

It was as if Hank's own little daughter had wandered out after midnight in the snow. Wandered out, looking for him. Little Celia, walking in her sleep.

But this child seemed wide awake. She marched towards him through the snow. She clutched the head of a green cloth snake under one arm. The snake's long body dragged after her. It left a trail in the snow.

The child stopped in front of Hank. It was the little girl from before, the girl in fur earmuffs. She was wearing them now. Snowflakes fell on her hair and on the shoulders of her coat. The white flakes stuck to her eyelashes. She blinked them away. "You're an elf, aren't you? A real elf." This was not a question. It was a statement. "You're one of Santa's helpers."

Hank gulped. What could he say but, "Yes"?

Then he stood up. He tried to keep the panic from his voice. "Honey, where do you live? Tell me where you live." He set the concertina on the chair.

"Did you tell Santa I've been good?" The girl still clutched the snake under her arm. A narrow red tongue dangled from its open jaw.

"Of course I did, of course." Hank looked up and down the sidewalk. No policeman walking his beat, no one to help.

"But I'm worried that Santa's not coming to our house. Mama says we can't have Christmas until Papa says sorry. She won't let him buy a Christmas tree."

"Well, sometimes it's hard to say sorry."

"But he *did*. He said he was sorry, 25 *times*."

Hank looked up and down the sidewalk at the falling snow. He would have to risk it, he would have to leave the lot unattended for a few minutes. Kneeling down in front of the child, he looked directly into her eyes. "Show me where you live. Take my hand and show me where."

She took his hand. She walked beside him, kicking at the snow with her bunny slippers. Her hand was so small in his. "Where now?" asked Hank. They'd turned the corner at Greenwich.

"This way." And she led him to the right, along Greenwich. Hank found himself near tears. Again he thought of his daughter Celia. Children are so strong. They do survive. They survive their parents' quarrels. They can even survive the divorce of their parents.

"Will you tell Santa again, that I've been good, and that Bubba's been good?"

"Yes, I will."

But what was he going to tell the child's parents? It was almost one o'clock in the morning. Hank would be a stranger ringing their doorbell. How could he explain that their daughter had left to find Santa's elf, and save Christmas for her family?

The snow fell silently all around them. The child led him to the left for a block, and then left again. She scuffed with her slippers through the several inches of fallen snow. And as she walked, she recited her wish list to Santa's elf. "...A doll house, and a doll carriage, and Bubba wants..."

Behind her, the green snake dragged a trail through the snow.

Then the child stopped short.

"Is this where you live?"

She nodded, silent. Harsh voices could be heard from within. The parents were still arguing.

Nick pushed open the low iron gate. Snow rode on top of the gate as it swung open, creaking.

The apartment was below the level of the sidewalk. Steps led down to a green door with a brass knocker. Hank's heart was in his throat. The child had a tight grip on his hand. What would the parent's think? Would they blame him? Would they have him arrested? Their loud voices could still be heard.

Hank reached out for the knocker. *Rap rap.*

"Who is it?" asked a woman's voice.

"It's your daughter," answered Hank. It was all he could think of to say, as his heart pounded.

The door opened a crack. "Sweetie! What are you doing out here? I thought you were in bed!"

The door opened wide. Both parents were now staring at Hank.

The mother had already pulled the child to her. "Who are you?" she asked in a cold voice.

"He's my elf."

"My name's Hank. I work at the Christmas tree lot, over at Greenwich and 7th." He was already backing away. "Your daughter, she came out to find me. She was worried about... well..."

"About what?" The woman's voice cut sharply.

Hank shrugged. "Just worried." He already had one foot on the stair behind him.

The father now took a step out the door towards him. "Look, Mister..."

Then Hank blurted, "She was worried that Santa Claus wouldn't come if you were fighting."

And he turned and climbed the steps, shutting the low gate behind him. Through the falling snow he was able to follow the snake's trail for a block. Then the trail faded, erased in the white. But by then Hank wasn't lost anymore, he knew where he was.

Throughout that night the garbage trucks tried to keep up with the falling snow, and failed. They'd been fitted with small snow blades, and could plow only a narrow swath. And the snow fell faster than they could clear it away.

Hank watched them try—and finally give up. He stood on the curb and watched the garbage trucks rumble away. It was 2:30 in the morning. The little girl with the earmuffs was surely safe in her bed. Again Hank's thoughts drifted to his own daughter, Celia, so far away. Two more days...

A delicious smell drew Hank back to the here-and-now. He ducked back into the hut, and checked the flame under the frying pan. He was roasting some chestnuts. He lifted the lid. With a knife he stabbed one of the chestnuts and lifted it out of the pan. He laid the chestnut on the table, and then tried to pick it up. "Ouch, ouch! Hot!" He was wearing gloves, but they had shortened fingers. He'd better let the chestnut cool off.

Hank didn't really like being alone on the night shift. These last weeks he'd been edgy, nervous. But the falling snow and its silence had a calming effect. He felt safer somehow. *No one is after me*, he told himself. He'd been telling himself this for weeks and it was probably true. But his conscience wouldn't leave him in peace.

Hank picked up the chestnut again—and jumped when a voice said, "Are those chestnuts I smell?"

It was a young face that peered in through the doorway of the hut. A face younger than Hank's by 15 years, and with a small trimmed mustache. The policeman couldn't have been more than 25. Hank knew that behind his back he held a nightstick. One of those hard-rubber batons that cracked open heads as easily as one cracked open a chestnut.

"Here, let me help. There's a trick to it." And the policeman stepped in, without being asked, without even a search warrant. "You just score the chestnut with your knife, like so." He looked into Hank's face. "That's some mustache you got. How long did it take to grow one like that?"

Hank fingered his handlebar mustache. He gave a nervous smile.

"Mind if I sit down?" The young policeman dropped to the only chair. It was the kitchen chair from the dumpster. "Nice little place you got here. Real cozy. Say…" He laid his nightstick across his knees and leaned forward. "That was nice work last week, you tackling that purse-snatcher."

Hank's eyes widened in surprise. "How did you know that?"

"Don't you remember? I was walking my beat, I saw the crowd gathered, and I asked someone exactly what they'd seen."

Ever since the cop had appeared in the doorway, Hank had hardly dared to breathe. He felt bottled up. "I… I can't take all the credit. My friend Glen, he…"

"Ah, go on, take the credit." The policeman pointed at the pan on the campstove. "You got any of those chestnuts to spare?"

Hank darted a nervous glance. "Sure, sure. Here, take…"

The cop stood up. "Two's fine. They'll keep my pockets warm. Well…" He tapped his baton against the brim of his cap in salute. "Merry Christmas."

"Merry Christmas." Hank repeated in a tense voice. He'd been holding his secret inside for so long. He felt as if he might burst if he didn't tell someone. "Wait!"

The policeman didn't turn around for a moment. When he did, he asked in a level voice, "What's the problem?"

Hank was flustered. "I… I have a confession to make."

"Do I look like a priest?" The young policeman stood there in his dark uniform.

"Yes… no!" Hank grew desperate. "It's just that you came

along when I needed... It's almost as if someone sent you to me. Please, just for a minute. Sit down again."

"I'm supposed to meet my partner up the street."

Hank looked down at his hands. He picked at a spot of pitch on his glove. When he finally spoke, he choked out his words. "I'm a coward. I saw something. And I didn't tell anyone, not anyone. I've felt sick inside ever since. I... I saw a murder happen." He voice dropped to a whisper. "I saw someone get killed."

The cop had taken a small notepad from an inside pocket of his jacket. "When?"

Hank drew a deep breath. He looked up. "December 1st. No, I guess it was the 2nd. It was about 3:30 in the morning."

"Where?"

"Across the street. I mean, the murder happened across the street. I was over on this side. I was standing down by the alley."

"What happened?"

"Well, there was a black limousine. It was parked in front of that jazz club over there."

"The Vanguard?" The policeman clicked his pen shut. He returned the notepad to its inner pocket.

Hank didn't notice. He continued in his confession. "The limousine's motor was running. I could see the exhaust coming out of the tailpipe." Hank picked and picked at his glove. He tried to keep his voice under control. "There was this strange sound. I thought... I thought it was an owl hooting. But it wasn't. There was a man pressed up against the wall. A gun was pointed at his head." Hank looked up at the policeman with pleading eyes. "For a second I thought it was a toy gun. I couldn't believe what I was seeing. But the man was crying in this strange way. He… he slid down the wall… he…"

Sobs jerked from Hank. He hid his face in his gloved hands.

"What is it? You want to be forgiven?"

Hank nodded into his hands.

"For what? For being in the wrong place at the wrong time?"

Hank protested. "But… but I was wrong! I should have gone straight to the police."

"You got that right. So…" The cop pulled out a card. "The next murder you see, give us a call."

"That's all?" Hank's tear-stained face wore a look of disbelief. "You're not going to arrest me, or deport me?"

"By the way, we made a couple of arrests in the case."

"What?!" Hank looked up, dazed.

"Don't you read the papers? Somebody called in the license plate on the limo. Some old guy with a pair of binoculars. An ex-cop." The policeman pointed with his baton. "Guy named Baxter. Lives right across the street, up on the third floor." He chuckled. "Once a cop, always a cop."

The policeman eyed the frying pan with its hot chestnuts. "I'll take a few more of those, if you don't mind. It's going to be a long, cold night."

Hank followed the policeman out to the sidewalk. "I've felt so terrible all this time. I've felt like a criminal myself."

"Give yourself a break. You remind me of my dad."

"I do?" Hank was taken aback. Did he look *that* old?

"Yeah, he gives himself a hard time. Hell, he gave *me* a hard time."

The following morning, buses and delivery trucks tried to proceed as if it was a normal day. Some were able to push their way through the foot of snow. Even a few yellow cabs struggled for a while, only to become stuck, or worse. A taxi slid sideways in slow-motion down 7th Avenue. Finally it bumped a lamppost.

Snow soon covered the empty cab. The snow covered everything in a blanket of white. The signal lights continued to change as the snow fell on the empty intersection. Yellow to red, red to green. But no one used the crosswalk. Instead, people crossed wherever they pleased, wading through the snow. They were trying to get to work. At least the subway trains were still moving.

Meanwhile, children had been playing in the snow since dawn. Glen waved to the kids and ducked their snowballs. He was using the broom to push a path down the sidewalk. Hank and Nick were busy shaking each Christmas tree free of snow. There were only about 60 trees left to sell. And then there was the giant balsam, the display tree. It blinked its coloured lights as the snow continued to fall.

By now the roof of the hut sagged dangerously. It was only a tarp, after all. Hank was elected to do the job. First he climbed up onto the roof of the van and cleared it of snow. From there he could reach over with the broom to the hut's roof. It was a dry, light snow. "Hey, Glen!" he called down. "This is perfect powder for skiing!"

When Hank finished, he tossed the broom down. But he didn't come down himself yet. He stood with his hands on his hips on top of the van, and drew in a deep breath. The weight of guilt was off his shoulders. From where he stood he could look up and down the street. He couldn't see far, because of the falling snow. But a wild happiness surged through him. The city was transformed. All traffic had now stopped. Everything was white, and silent. The silence was like a blessing fallen from heaven. Only human voices could be heard. Someone waved up at him. He waved back. He could have stayed up there forever. The aroma of Nick's coffee brewing is what finally drew him down from his perch.

The three men were inside drinking their coffee when Jennifer stopped by. "Hi, guys. I'm in a hurry."

Jennifer had wrapped herself, head and shoulders, in a huge black shawl. Snowflakes covered the top of her head, white on black. Her smile held what everyone's smile held: wonder and disbelief. "Isn't this great?" She licked snowflakes from her cheek. "I just came by to give you these." She was digging in her shoulder bag. She pulled out a pair of battered toe shoes. Their dirty ribbons dangled. The shoes were no longer pink, but a greyish pink.

Glen accepted the toe shoes with both hands as if they were precious relics.

"And to give you these." Jennifer held up two tickets. "They're for today's matinee."

Glen tilted his head and read the labels on the tickets. "*The Nutcracker.* Holy cow! This is the ballet you've been rehearsing for?"

Jennifer grinned. "I'm one of the Sugarplum fairies. Didn't I tell you?" She pressed the tickets into Glen's hand. "Here, take them. I'm sorry that I could only get two." She glanced quickly over at Nick and Hank. Who would be using the other ticket?

Nick had a teasing look in his dark eyes. "So, Glennie, you gonna take your friend?"

"Ahh," said Jennifer, raising her eyebrows. She turned towards Glen. "What friend?"

Glen still held the toe shoes in one hand and the tickets in the other. He was blushing. "But what about Hank?"

Hank was busy. He was waxing the wooden skis that Texas Eddy had sold him. He was using a candle stub, rubbing it along the underside of each ski. His face was glowing with anticipation. He paused, looking up.

"Jennifer, do you know where I can find a toy store around here?"

"A toy store? No, not around here. But there's always F.A.O. Schwarz."

"Do they have good stuff? I need a special present. It's for my little daughter. I promised her a Christmas present from New York. A special one."

Jennifer laughed. "Trust me. It's up on 58th Street and Madison. You can take the subway."

But Hank didn't take the subway. He took 7th Avenue.

He placed the two skis down on the snowy sidewalk and stepped into them. Leaning over, he wrapped the leather bindings around his hiking boots. At each ankle he buckled the bindings and then straightened up. "Can you hand me my knapsack, Nicki?"

The knapsack was empty for now. Hank slipped his arms through the straps.

"Wait!" Nick waved an old sock. "You forgot this." From the sock Nick pulled out a $50 bill and a $20 bill. "You can pay the kitty back tomorrow when we get our month's wage."

"Hey, Hank!" Glen called over. He was busy pulling a tree through the tree wrapper. "Where are your ski poles?"

Hank pulled his Canada hat down over his ears. He lifted up a leg and took a step-turn, one ski now pointing north. Then he lifted up his other leg and brought that ski around. "I'll have to do without poles," he called over his shoulder. And he set off.

Hank soon got a rhythm going, swinging his arms. His skis glided forward—first one, then the other. It was the greatest of freedoms. He was skiing north up a one-way street going south! He couldn't wipe the smile from his face. Falling snowflakes whitened his eyebrows and mustache. His legs moved under him, the skis gliding. "Coming through!" he called out to a group of children ahead. They'd made a snowman right in the middle of 7th Avenue.

Hank ducked a snowball, and another.

The children reminded him of that little girl last night, dragging her green snake through the snow. Her small worried face framed with earmuffs had haunted him ever since. Would she have a Christmas? Or would she always remember the year that Santa didn't come?

Up at 29th Street, Hank got his second wind. He squinted through the falling snow.

At 58th Street he glided in a wide turn. He slowed a bit, calling to a policeman on horseback, "Officer, could you direct me to a store called F.A.O. Schwarz?"

An arm pointed, "Three blocks over. Can't miss it."

No, there was certainly no way to miss it. On the corner of 5th Avenue, glass walls reached up three stories. Coloured lights were strung high across the glass in the shape of Santa and his reindeer.

Inside, a 50-foot Christmas tree sparkled with lights and coloured balls. Hank had left his skis outside. They were in the care of a corner Santa Claus, who was ringing a bell for charity. Hank had brushed the snow off his arms and shaken out his hat. Now he stood looking up at the tree. Slowly the giant tree turned in a circle, showing off its lights and candy canes and tinsel. *If only Celia could see this.*

Children swarmed everywhere. Excitement seemed to pulse in the air. Hank began to wander the aisles. Children dodged around his legs. Their excited chatter and shouts filled the huge toy store.

Hank walked slowly on, trying to take it all in. He never wanted to leave. His eyes lit up as he gazed around in wonder. He was like a child himself. But an adult voice in his head told him that he couldn't stay long. He had to get back to the Christmas tree lot.

Then he spotted the perfect gift for Celia.

It was a music box, with a ballerina poised on top. Someone had wound up the key before wandering away. Now the music tinkled as the ballerina slowly turned round and round. She turned on one leg, on a pointed toe shoe. Her net skirt sparkled. The crown on her head sparkled. Even the ballerina's eyelashes sparkled.

It was perfect. Hank imagined Celia unwrapping such a gift. He would show her how to twist the key. Her face would light up as she listened to the tinkling tune. And her eyes would shine as she watched the ballerina twirl slowly round and round.

Glen was ready for his date. "How do I look?" He turned slowly around in front of Nick. "Is the haircut too short?" He smoothed his hands back over his ears.

"Relax, Glennie. You look great."

Glen looked down at his sweater with fondness. "This sweater brought Magda and me together," he murmured. "I'll have to tell my sister. She knit it, you know."

"Yeah, I know, Glennie."

Glen pulled on his Christmas hat with the earflaps.

A visitor appeared in the doorway. It was Lucky's owner. "Mmmm, do I smell after-shave lotion?" The bulldog strained at his leash to come in. There was snow on top of Lucky's little leather coat. He now wore a black leather cap as well, and black booties on all four paws.

His owner held out a bottle tied with a bow. "Wine from France. It's your Christmas present from Lucky and me." Then he looked Glen over, and whistled, even though Glen wasn't his type. "So, you going on a date? Who's the lucky guy?"

"Don't tease him," said Nick, holding the bottle of wine. And to Glen he said, "You got your tickets, right? Yeah, that's good, you look fine, relax, man."

Glen hurried over to the Quik-Stop Dry Cleaners. Magda let him in. Then she locked the door behind him.

Glen grinned at her. His hat hung over his ears. "Are you ready?"

But she'd turned her back to him. "You tell me only we are going somewhere special. You don't tell me where." She pulled down the shade on the front door.

"It's a surprise," explained Glen. He followed her as she pulled down the shades on each of the front windows. Then she turned to look up at him. She spoke quietly. "A surprise, it makes me worried. I don't like surprises. I had too many of these in my life." She continued to hold his gaze. "Soon you will go away, Glen Turner. You will go back to your village in the mountains."

They were alone in the shop. No one else had come in to work that day, because of the snow. Only Magda had come in for a few hours that morning, and now she was closing.

Glen stood looking down at her, his shoulders hunched. "Let's not think about me leaving. That's not till tomorrow. I'm still here now."

"One of us must think of it, and be sad for us both." Her dark eyes were steady. Then she reached for the mop that leaned against the counter.

"But there are *good* surprises, Magda." Without thinking, Glen took the mop from her hands. He began wiping up the melted snow on the floor.

As she watched him, Magda couldn't help but smile. "Yes, I remember. You came to bring your sweater here. You wanted to cause no extra trouble for me. You talked fast. You waved your arms."

Glen straightened from his mopping. "Were you laughing at me then?"

Magda looked at him. Then she lowered her eyes, suddenly shy. "I saw you were a good person."

Glen blushed. "So you had your eye on me, and I didn't even know it?" His meaty hands gripped the mop handle. "I read something in a magazine once. The article claimed that it's always the woman who chooses the man." Glen waited. "So that's true?"

Magda kept her head down. "I believe it is not the man or the woman who chooses," she murmured. Her fingers found the small gold cross at her throat. She raised the cross to her lips. "I believe it is someone else." She lifted her gaze. They looked at each other in mutual shyness.

A sharp knock rapped at the door. Glen and Magda both held their breath. Another sharp rap sounded. Glen and Magda held still.

"Do you like pizza?" Glen whispered. He stared intently at Magda. He waited for her answer as if it were of the highest importance. When she didn't say anything, he added in a whisper, "I own a pizza place, back home."

Magda whispered back. "You told me this."

"I did?" Glen hissed.

"Where you live in Canada, it is very far from here."

They were still whispering.

"It's not as far as Peru."

"I am not going back to Peru."

Glen was sweating now.

Magda nodded towards the door. "The customer, he is gone now. We can talk."

But Glen was looking down at his shoes. Thoughts flew through his head.

He began mopping the floor again, as fast as he could. The mop was getting too wet to be of use. Glen straightened up. "Magda, I'm a bachelor."

"What is that?"

"I've never been married. I've never... lived with a woman." Glen's cheeks flushed.

Magda regarded him for a long moment.

Then she drew a low stool out from the corner. "Please, come to sit here. I will show you how it is to live with a woman."

Glen hesitated. "You're making fun of me."

Magda simply waited, looking up at him with her dark, wide-set eyes.

Glen leaned the mop against the wall. "Are you sure?" He sat down carefully on the little stool. He took off his hat. "Now what?"

"Now I sit to your lap."

Glen tugged his sweater down over his stomach. Magda had to

stand on tiptoe to sit on his lap. Her weight settled on his thighs. She slipped her arms around his bulk and leaned her head against his chest. Glen's arms had no place to go but around her soft warm body.

They sat like that for some time. Magda's ear was pressed against his chest as he held her. "I hear your heart," she murmured. After a while, she added, "Your heart loves you. It is beating for you."

Glen felt touched, and surprised. "What a strange thing to say."

"The thought comes to me just now, when I listen."

Again they grew quiet. Outside, there was no traffic noise, only voices of people passing by. A shovel could be heard scraping across a sidewalk.

Glen bent his head. He could smell the scent of Magda's black hair. And he could see a few silver hairs threaded through the black. *I'm holding a woman in my lap. I'm holding Magda.* Every lonely cell in his body was absorbing her warmth. He pressed his lips to the top of her head.

Magda murmured something, her head against his chest.

"What did you say?"

She didn't answer. But what she had murmured into his sweater was, "Thank you, Saint Jude."

In the darkened theater, Glen and Magda sat holding hands. Children surrounded them. Every seat in the New York State Theater was filled for the matinee.

Children had come to see *The Nutcracker* with their parents, or with older brothers and sisters. An entire dancing class sat with their teacher in the rows in front of Glen and Magda. But no one made a peep. All eyes looked to the stage and its magic. All eyes sparkled, reflecting the lights and colour of what was being seen. Everyone gave themselves over to the fantasy of the ballet.

Glen and Magda sat leaning towards each other, their shoulders touching. Glen had slumped down in his seat. He didn't want to block the view of the small child behind him. Every once in a while Glen had to wipe his sweaty hand on his pants. But he always took Magda's hand into his own again, and gave it a little squeeze.

A group of ballerinas was now at centre stage. The dancers were all very thin, but with strong muscular legs. And they all wore the same kind of short, sparkling costume. With perfect timing they lifted to the points of their pink satin toe shoes. All together their graceful arms rose above their heads.

It was "The Dance of the Sugarplum Fairies."

On their way back to the subway, Glen and Magda walked in happy silence. He'd tucked her arm under his own. They walked at her slower pace. Once she slipped on the snow and fell against him and he caught her. "Are you all right?"

"Yes, I am fine." But she held more tightly to his arm. Then as they passed a low stone wall, she pointed. "I would like you to help me up."

Glen stopped. "What for?"

"Do not ask that question. Just help me, please." She began to brush off the snow from the stones.

"Here, let me do that."

Then Glen turned to face her. He put his hands under her arms. "Are you sure?"

She nodded—and was lifted up. Glen held her there, afraid she might slip. "Now can I set you down?"

Magda shook her head. "Not yet." Her face was level with his. She was looking directly into his eyes. "It is time for us to kiss." She spoke calmly, in a matter-of-fact voice.

Glen's heart pounded. "Is it?"

Magda nodded, solemn.

He moved closer. He now held her around the waist. It was strange to have her be so tall. Her kind dark eyes stared into his. Glen blushed. "You have to close your eyes first."

She closed them, and waited.

Glen looked into her face: her wide cheekbones, her full mouth, her smooth, brown skin. She was offering herself to him. And at that moment, his heart seemed to crack wide open in his chest. He loved her. He loved her with all his heart. Magda, this strange, calm woman from Peru.

He closed his own eyes, and his lips found hers. Warm, so warm and soft, as the snow fell around them.

Mr. Baxter

After that terrible night in 1962, Lew Baxter and his new wife had not celebrated Christmas.

Nor had they celebrated the next. And by the following Christmas, his wife had left. She'd given up on him. "It's your pride, Lew. You can't bear the thought that you're not the perfect cop. You think you failed in your duty. But what about your duty to me? I'm your wife. Can't you just forgive yourself for what happened that night?"

But Lew Baxter had turned away from her.

Why had those two children been out on an icy fire escape at eight o'clock at night? What God in heaven would let that happen?

But he couldn't blame God. It was a matter of human error. His own error. Looking up at the fire escape that freezing night, he'd seen the second child slip and fall. Keeping his head back, Lew had set the first child to the sidewalk. Then he'd stepped backwards, trying to judge where to stand so that he could catch this second child that now hurtled down.

And that's when he'd slipped on the ice.

7

CHRISTMAS EVE

It was now past four in the morning, in the first early hours of Christmas Eve. The snow seemed to be stopping at last. Only a few stray flakes drifted down. The sidewalk was freshly swept. Nick was sitting on a box on the sidewalk, playing his pan-flute, when a man walked up.

"Excuse me, but I can't sleep." The tall, gaunt man stood with his hands in the pockets of his overcoat. "I can't sleep with you playing that flute."

Nick looked up. It was that tall, thin, bitter man with sores on his face. The man who'd demanded their best and biggest Christmas tree, since he wouldn't be alive by the New Year.

Nick stood up and slipped the pan-flute into his jacket pocket. His grey hair was braided, with black ribbons hanging down. The lines in his handsome face appeared deeper at this hour, in this light. He pointed towards the hut. "You wanna come inside, where it's warmer?"

"No, I like it out here."

"Okay, just give me a minute, I'll get you the chair."

Nick set the kitchen chair down in the middle of the sidewalk. "Sorry if I kept you awake, man."

His guest sat down. He pulled his long coat around him.

Nick sat down again on his box. "Yeah, man, it's good you came along. I was just sitting here feeling sorry for myself. I guess you could tell by my music."

"Oh?" The string of bare light bulbs was directly overhead. Harsh shadows hollowed the man's bony face.

It was hard for Nick to look into that face for any length of time. It was a face so thin that it showed the skull underneath. And the skin was covered with those open sores. It was like looking into a death mask. It made him feel uneasy.

Nick looked briefly away. "Man, there's something wrong here. Maybe I'm not so smart. I don't know a lot of big words yet. But I know when things ain't right."

Nick felt weighed down with the world's concerns, and his own. His talk began to ramble. "Here in New York, they got dogs dressed better than people." He pointed to the corner. "I've seen more than one fellow eating out of that trash can. And I met a girl here, a dancer, she starves herself to be thin."

The Christmas lights blinked on and off. They flashed their colours onto the surrounding snow.

Nick stood up. He began to pace. It was past four in the

morning. It was a time when dark thoughts could accumulate. And now those dark thoughts spilled out, to a stranger. "What am I doing here? I been selling these trees. They get cut down, and a week after Christmas they're hauled away in a garbage truck." Nick paused in his pacing. "Here's what I said to myself. 'Nicki, you're gonna bring nature into the city, right to the people.' Why, a kid living here, he only knows about pavement. He don't know about the soil."

Nick sat down on his box again. He looked down at his hands in their ragged gloves with their shortened fingers. "Every day I get pitch on me from these trees. When you cut them, the pitch comes out. It's like having their blood on my hands. I dunno..."

Nick was quiet for a moment. Then he looked up, directly into his guest's gaunt face. He could bear it only for a moment, before looking away. "So what do you think's the matter with me? You think I'm lovesick?"

"Aren't we all?"

"Yeah, I'm caught, man. I'm caught. There's this woman, Kate. She's got herself engaged to another guy..." Nick's husky voice dropped even lower. "You think maybe I should give up on her?"

It was that time of early morning when strangers talk to each other, telling each other about their lives.

"Kate and me, we've got this connection, right? My brains might not be so quick as hers, but we got this connection, heart to heart. But when I called her, she hung up on me. And then I sent her a letter..." Nick sighed. Then he dared another glance at the man's face. "Hey man, you cold? You're shivering. Let's go in."

Nick lit a second candle inside the hut. "I use candles instead of the lamp." He blew out the match. "Reminds me of home."

The candlelight was kind to Nick's guest. It softened the hollows of his cheeks. His eyes burned dark in their sockets. He stared at the flame. "My lover is in the hospital, over at Saint Vincent's." The man pressed his lips together. "He's dying." And he lifted a bony hand and waved at his own face with its terrible sores.

"I see," Nick nodded. "So that's why you can't sleep. It wasn't my flute keeping you awake so much." Nick then sat on the edge of the table. He rubbed his hands over his face, trying to wipe it all away. "Yeah, I was over at Saint Vinny's. I took a couple of trees over. I was asking about this AIDS business. Damn," he cursed under his breath. "Even little kids, they need blood, the blood is bad, they end up sick with this thing. It ain't right. Hey, you want a blanket around your shoulders? I got a blanket in the van… No?"

"I'm always cold now." The man hesitated, then spoke again. "I've been wondering. Do you really believe aloe vera would help?" And he pointed to the sores on his face. "I saw a tube of aloe vera cream in a health food store."

"Okay, that's the spirit! But your best bet is to buy an aloe plant. You cut a little piece off, open it up. Inside, there's gonna be this jelly stuff. You just smear on a little." Nick lowered his voice to a husky whisper. "One thing though…"

"What's that?" Nick's guest leaned forward.

"Before you cut, you talk to the plant a little, tell him what you're gonna do. You talk, you explain. Then the plant is more willing to do you a good turn." Nick parted two fingers and worked them like a scissors. "Just take a little snip each time."

Clackety-clackety, clackety-clackety. The sound quickly rose to a muffled roar under them.

"My god! You live right over the subway trains!"

"Yeah," Nick shouted. "After a while you don't notice the noise."

The roar died away. In the snowy silence, Nick slowly nodded. "Yeah..." Then his voice softened. "So how's your wolf?"

"My wolf?"

"Yeah, your Fraser fir, your Christmas tree. You got it all decorated? Lights and everything?"

"Oh!" The man's face brightened. "Yes, everything. I strung cranberries and popcorn. It took me hours. Very old-fashioned. Oh! And I found some angel hair in a secondhand store. Five boxes of it, from the 50's." He hesitated. "Do you know about angel hair?"

"Sure, man, I know about angel hair. What I remember is scratching a lot afterwards. I'm telling you, that stuff was itchy." Nick stood up, walking over to the doorway of the little hut. "You're gonna have to tell me your boyfriend's name, so's I can take some fir branches over to him at St. Vinny's. Some Balsam branches. They'll smell his room up real nice." Nick looked out from the doorway. "I'll be darned. It's snowing again." A smile spread on his face. "...Yeah, angel hair. My mother, she always had us kids drape it on the tree, last thing. Looked real pretty."

"Yes, isn't it beautiful? It's like a white web spun all over the tree.

And the coloured lights shine through." His own eyes shone. "Each light shines through with a halo around it." He was staring at the candle flame. "Do you think that's why they call it angel hair?"

By daylight, it was still snowing. Nick walked through falling snow over to the Deli. He was on his way to buy the morning's coffee beans. But he didn't have the usual bounce in his step. He kept thinking about the fellow from the night before, and shaking his head.

And he kept thinking about Kate. Beautiful, smart Kate. It was time to give up hope. She wasn't coming back to him. He'd lost her.

The streets were still unplowed. Crossing Greenwich, a path was worn through the snow. It was a narrow path. People had to step out of the way to let each other pass. By now, Nick had made friends in the neighbourhood, and he stopped to talk to each one. On a normal day they would have been in a hurry, but not today, not with the snow.

Nick wiped the soles of his moccasins on the doormat. This was usually the favorite moment of his day: when he opened the door to Harry's Deli. The aroma of fresh-roasted coffee would soon fill his senses.

Inside, customers stood in line at the counter. It seemed as if everyone was talking at once in happy chatter. The subject was the snow, of course.

An elderly woman turned to Nick. "This must be like Canada for you."

Nick nodded. "Yeah, ain't it beautiful?"

Finally it was Nick's turn. From behind the counter, Harry glared at him. "The usual, I suppose." He weighed out an eighth of a pound of French roast and poured the beans into the grinder. Then he tossed in a pinch of Mexican beans. "Oh yeah, you got a call here yesterday. You're Nick, right? From Canada?" The machine whirred noisily.

Nick's heart lifted. "Oh yeah?"

Harry poured the ground coffee into a small paper sack and folded it closed. "It was a woman who called. Said she'd call back today, same time. Next?" Harry looked to the customer behind Nick.

"When? What time did she call?"

"What time?" Harry turned towards the rear of the Deli. He called to his wife. "Ma! What time did that lady call from Canada?"

"Don't ask me. Around nine yesterday morning, I guess."

Harry turned back to Nick. "You hear that?" He began measuring out coffee beans for the next customer. "But don't talk long. I don't want my phone tied up. This is a business I run here."

Nick returned to the Deli within the hour. He was early by a few minutes. He stood to one side of the cash register, and eyed the phone. But he couldn't keep still, and he couldn't keep a grin off his face.

He jumped when the phone finally rang. But it wasn't Kate. He handed the receiver over to Harry.

Harry wiped his hands on his apron. "Next time, I'll answer the phone in my own store."

When the phone rang again, Harry didn't answer right away. It rang three times, four times. Nick moved from foot to foot in a nervous dance. His hand itched to reach over and pick up that phone. Now it was ringing for the fifth time. "Yeah, man," he muttered, "it's gotta be her, it's Kate, calling me." He was just about to grab it when Harry reached over with a weary sigh. "Harry's Deli."

Nick watched Harry's face intently.

"Yeah, just a minute." Harry held out the phone's receiver. "It's for you. Just keep it short."

Nick cradled the receiver in both hands. "Hey, it's me, Nicki." His voice was a husky croon. "I been missing you, baby… You got my letter? Yeah? Well, I had Hank help me a little with the spelling… You believe it. Every word. You been in my heart… What?" Nick's eyes lit up. He grinned with relief. "You do? But what about the other guy?… You called it off?"

"Time's up!" bellowed Harry.

Nick pressed the phone receiver to his ear. "What?… Yeah. But how'd you know to call here at the Deli?… I mentioned it in my letter?… Yeah, I come in here every morning. The coffee here, man, it's the best. This guy, he mixes me a special blend. I'll bring back a pound… Yeah, whole beans, I know… Yeah. All right. So what are you doin' awake? It's gotta be six in the morning out where you are… Oh yeah, Calgary, that's only two hours earlier than here…"

Harry waved his arm at Nick. "Hang up!" But his wife was at his side. "Let him be, Harry. It's Christmas Eve."

"Yeah, it's Christmas Eve, and customers will be wanting to call in their orders."

Nick plugged his other ear with his finger as he talked into the phone. "We got some controversy here… I said, con-tro-ver-sy. That means when people are having a difference of opinion." Nick laughed. "Yeah, like you and me. But that's all gonna change." He turned to look at the steamed-up window of the Deli as he listened. "Yeah, how'd you know? We got over three feet now, and it's still snowing."

Hank and Glen and Nick sipped their wine. They were standing outside the hut. It was nine o'clock at night on Christmas Eve. The rush was over. The sidewalks were deserted. And the streets were covered with four feet of snow—snow that had finally stopped.

It was a clear night. Church bells rang out from up on 7th Avenue.

"To the boss." Hank held up a cup with a broken handle.

"To the boss," repeated Glen and Nick.

Hank wiped his mustache with the back of his hand. "Not bad." They were drinking the red wine given to them by Lucky's owner. Hank took another sip and smacked his lips.

Their full month's wage lay on the table inside the hut: $9,000. All cash.

"To New York," Nick toasted.

Glen raised his cup. "And to Peru," he added, with a shy smile. He'd said nothing to them yet about what had happened, about the kiss.

Hank's eyes were teasing. "So Glennie, tell us, what's with your friend Magda?"

Glen blushed as his smile spread to a grin. "Well, we're serious."

Hank's jaw dropped. "You mean, *serious?*"

Glen blushed even redder.

Nick chuckled to himself and murmured, "Man, he don't look serious to me. He looks happy. That's good. Yeah, that's good." Then he tipped back his head and looked up at the sky. "To you, Kate. Kate o' my heart." And he lifted his cup of wine in a silent toast. Then he added, "And to Frank Sinatra, wherever you are, man."

The snowstorm had cleared the air. There was a faint glitter of stars in the sky over New York.

Red wine was again being poured from the bottle. Three battered cups without handles were filled again.

"Mmm," murmured Hank. "This warms me right up."

Church bells rang out once more in the snowy silence.

"What do you guys think?" asked Glen. "Shall we start taking down the shelter? No one's been by for the last half hour."

"A toast to our little house!" cried Hank.

"How many trees left?" Nick counted. "Looks like five."

"What about the big one?"

The three men turned, to look up at the tall fir. The display tree still blinked its coloured lights.

A woman's high voice called out. "Are we too late? I hope we're not too late." The woman had her family in tow. She pulled her husband along. A boy followed behind them, holding his little sister by the hand—a little sister wearing fur earmuffs.

The woman arrived out of breath. "We just came from Christmas Eve service over at the church. We need a tree. It's all my fault. I've been horrid. I always get horrid at Christmas time. I just get into a funk. I'm afraid I've made my family suffer once again." She looked around at the trees that were left. "Is this all you have, these short ones? How much are they?" She turned to her husband. "What do you think? Which one?"

Shrugging his shoulders, he smiled wearily. "Honey, whatever you want."

"I'm not sure… Oh!" The woman caught her breath. "Is… is that one for sale?" And she pointed up at the display tree.

Her husband's voice cut in. "I'm afraid that's beyond our budget."

The woman gazed up at the tree with longing. "Yes, of course it is." She lowered her gaze. And finally she turned, and looked directly at Hank. Her face flushed with embarrassment. "You're the one who brought my daughter home the other night."

The husband also seemed embarrassed. He held out his hand to Hank. "We want to thank you again."

The woman's face twisted. "When I think what might have happened to her…"

"Sir?" called Glen. "I think we can let that tree go for..." He turned to Nick. "Thirty dollars?"

"Whatever you say, Glennie."

"That price includes the Christmas lights and the stand," added Hank.

The husband protested. "You can't be serious." He looked up at the balsam fir. "That must be a $150 tree, at the least! And the lights too?"

It took both Hank and Glen to deliver the tree. Glen carried the butt of the giant fir on his shoulder, and Hank followed behind, holding up the crown with one hand. The strings of coloured lights were still wound round and round the huge fir.

Hank's other hand had been quietly taken by the little girl. She walked beside her elf, with the tail of her snake trailing after.

"Here we are!" cried the woman at the low iron gate.

It was a struggle. The giant fir tilted down three narrow steps from the sidewalk. It squeezed through a doorway and down a hall. The children followed the tree's progress with wide eyes.

Glen lowered the butt in its stand to the living room floor. Then he walked the tree upright. The very tiptop brushed the high ceiling.

"It fits!" cried the boy. He hurried over with the end of the cord to plug it in. The lights blinked on. The giant fir filled the room with its fragrance.

The small girl stared up at the dazzle of coloured lights. She still gripped Hank's hand. She wouldn't let it go. "We need a star," she murmured.

"There," he said, and proudly held out a star. It was a gold star, with all its sharp points of light.

Back at the hut, Nick stuffed three $100 bills into the old sock on the shelf. That would pay their electric bill at the Chinese restaurant. The rest of the $9,000 now warmed his ankles. He wore the bills inside his high moccasins, laced up tight with leather thongs.

Nick tried a little test jump, and danced from foot to foot. It seemed all right. All he had to do was to walk natural. Natural and relaxed. No big deal. No one would guess that he was wearing $9,000. He grinned down at his ankles. "Yeah, man, this is some trip."

He lifted his battered cup from the table and drained the last of his wine.

Then he took a last look around the hut. His glance lingered on the garlic braid, half-gone, that hung from a post. And the little mirror leaning on the shelf. The wooden liquor cabinet. The rug. The heater. The lamp. In an hour or two, this homey little place would be gone, torn down.

But he couldn't bear to do it alone. He'd wait for Hank and Glen to get back.

Outside, he picked up the broom. The sidewalk didn't really need sweeping. There was only a last skiff of snow. And no one was around to drop a candy wrapper or a cigarette butt. It was 10 o'clock at night on Christmas Eve. Everyone had gone home to celebrate. Even the church bells were quiet. Nick could hear the clicking of the signal lights at the intersection. They directed only ghost traffic.

But Texas Eddy was no ghost. Here he came, shuffling down the sidewalk.

"I worried you-all might have left already."

"Hey, not without saying good-bye, right?"

Eddy hitched up the pack on his back. He took a deep drag from his cigarette and pried it from his lip. "You need anything more? I won't charge. It'll be a gift."

Nick put his hand on Eddy's shoulder. "Stick around. We gotta take apart this little house of ours. You can have most everything in it. Whadda you say?"

Eddy lifted his glance to the hut's roof. "What about that blue tarp?"

"It's yours, Eddy. It's yours."

Eddy grinned, teeth missing. He ran his hand back over his matted red hair. He seemed at a loss for words. Then he muttered, "You know, I've been thinking about what you said."

Nick leaned an ear close. "What was that?"

"About going back to Texas."

Nick grinned. "Oh yeah?"

Eddy's pale eyes wandered off. He was looking around at the silent, snow-filled streets. He wiped his nose on the sleeve of his army jacket. "It's just so pretty here." He took another deep drag from his cigarette and blew out a stream of smoke.

Nick choked, coughing. "Hey, man, you gotta blow that stuff the other way. Phew!" Then he tugged at Eddy's sleeve. "Come on, let's go check this out," and he nodded towards Greenwich Avenue.

Two teenagers were kicking a hacky-sack back and forth under the streetlamp at the corner. They wore only T-shirts and jeans and running shoes.

Without a word, Nick joined them in their game. He was light on his feet, hitting the little leather sac with the side of his ankle. The hacky-sack arced into the air. One of the teenagers caught it with a thrust of his knee.

Eddy had propped himself against the lamppost to watch. He hadn't had enough sleep the night before. His eyes were half-closed. He seemed to be dozing as he called out to Nick in a sleepy voice. "You-all gonna play your flute tonight before you go?"

"Yeah, one last time, just for you Eddy. But I'm busy here now."

On the sidewalk cleared of snow, Nick and the two teenagers hopped back and forth. The small leather sac leapt in the air from one to another of the players.

Nick's wide grin lit up his face. He danced back and forth in his high moccasins, the $9,000 warming his ankles.

He was almost out of breath when something red caught his eye. A red coat. A woman was walking across Greenwich, along the path dug through the snow. She was a beautiful woman. Nick appreciated beautiful women. "Whoa!" he gasped, kicking the hacky-sack back to one of the teenagers.

The woman had long, thick reddish brown hair. Her short red coat swung around her as she approached. She wore red lipstick the colour of her coat.

"I don't believe it," Nick gasped. He stopped short. The hacky-sack sailed past him and fell to the sidewalk. "Kate? Kate, is that you? Am I seein' things?"

She was a small, trim woman. She stepped up to the curb and came towards him. She was smiling, watching his reaction.

Nick hadn't moved. He squeezed his eyes shut, and opened them again as she stepped into his arms. She fit perfectly.

"Kate? But how'd you get here, with all this snow? I was just talkin' with you this morning, and now..." Nick whistled low. "Man, this is like a miracle."

Kate tilted her head back, smiling into Nick's face. "I took a plane, and a helicopter, and the subway. It's not a miracle. It's called 'money.' "

Then she looked over her shoulder. "Who's that old man? He seems to know you."

The man was coming across 7th Avenue, taking slow careful steps. He waved his cane. "Wait!" he called.

Kate looked back at Nick. Her eyes sparkled. "I've reserved a room for us at the Plaza Hotel."

The man with the cane called from the curb in a hoarse voice. "Wait! I'm going to buy a Christmas tree." But now he hesitated at the corner curb. He was looking down at his feet, unsure.

Texas Eddy saw this. He'd been leaning against the lamppost at the corner with his eyes half-shut. But now he woke up enough to reach out a helping hand. He braced the older man's elbow and steadied him as he stepped from the street up onto the sidewalk.

"Thank you," the man muttered, as if embarrassed to need

help. He walked towards Nick and Kate with slow and careful steps. He seemed quite concerned about slipping. He cast a glance at the teenagers, hopping back and forth on the snowy sidewalk.

Then he nodded to Nick. "I've heard you playing your flute, this last month."

Nick grinned. "Oh yeah?"

"Yes, I..." The older man looked away for a moment, as if embarrassed. "I seem to be buying a Christmas tree." Then he turned back to Nick. "Am I too late?"

Nick still held Kate in her red coat tightly in his arms. His low chuckle was for her. He looked into her eyes. "Hey, no, man, you're not too late."

Then he called over his shoulder to the corner. "Hey, Eddy, you do me a favor, man?"

Eddy's eye's flicked open. He'd been dozing again at the lamp-post. Now he slowly came to join them. A lit cigarette butt hung from his lip.

"This here is Texas Eddy, he's a friend of mine. He's gonna carry your tree home for you." Nick grinned. "Am I right, Eddy?"

Eddy smiled, showing his missing teeth. "Sure."

The man with the cane looked Eddy up and down. Then he nodded. "That would be very kind of you."

"Eddy's a good man. He'll take good care of you, just tell him where you live."

"I live up there, across 7th." And the man pointed his cane towards the building across the street. He pointed to the window above the sign that read "With Pain, or Without Pain." Again he looked Eddy over, as if doubting his strength. "I live on the third floor."

"Hey, Eddy," Nick called. "Take any of those trees over by the fence. He's got his pick. They're free tonight." Nick was now being tugged down the sidewalk by Kate. He said, "Babe, I gotta tear down this hut first, me and the boys."

Meanwhile, Eddy lifted one of the small balsam firs to his shoulder. "Let's go."

Eddy and the man with the cane now started across 7th Avenue. Snow was piled high on either side of the path.

"I don't really need this cane to walk," said the man. "I only use it when the streets are slippery."

Eddy said nothing. He seemed happy to be carrying the tree, happy and proud. The fragrant branches brushed against his cheek and neck.

The older man kept his eye on the path, checking for ice or any slippery patch. He shook his head. "That smell, of a Christmas tree, it brings back painful memories."

"Yeah," nodded Eddy, as if they were in agreement. "It's a nice smell."

"I don't really like Christmas," muttered the man with the cane.

"I liked Christmas when I was a kid," said Eddy, and drew in a deep puff from his cigarette.

They were now halfway across 7th. The corner streetlights shone down on their two figures, and on the quivering green branches of the fir.

"I must be crazy, getting this tree. I don't know what came over me, after all these years."

Eddy turned his head, peering through the branches of the fir. "You got a cigarette?"

The old man turned to look at Eddy. "But you're already smoking a cigarette."

"I am?" Eddy murmured. "Oh yeah." And with his tongue he flicked the cigarette butt from his lip. The glowing butt landed in a snowbank with a sizzle.

"That fellow called you 'Texas Eddy.' "

Eddy grinned, nodding, "Yeah, he's a funny guy." By now Eddy had offered his arm to the man.

Lew Baxter leaned on it for support. "My mother came from Texas," he murmured.

"Oh yeah? Whereabouts?"

And the two men proceeded at a slow, careful pace to the far curb.